AN ERA OF ERROR

Kass Ghayouri

ISBN: 1482799804

ISBN 13: 9781482799804

Library of Congress Control Number: 2013905250

CreateSpace Independent Publishing Platform

North Charleston, South Carolina

Dedication

This novel is dedicated to my sons,
Shahrooz and Omid Ghayouri,
who believe that this is my walk down memory lane.

Acknowledgement

Foremost, I am obliged to acknowledge a dominant figure and most influential leader in the South African liberation movement, Nelson Mandela. He stood in the path of tyranny and injustice to dismantle the apartheid system. Additionally, I pay tribute to Mahatma Gandhi, who played a prominent role in the eradication of discrimination against Indians in South Africa.

I am indebted to my son Shahrooz, who dedicated his time as I hurdled all the obstacles in completing my task. This novel would have remained a dream had it not been for my son Omid; his patience made my creation possible. I share the credit of my work with my students, who served me as I plodded through this difficult process. Taanya, Nishaani, Pavithra, Kalaisan, Harrish, and Mathula, it is with your help that we have grown multifold. I owe my deepest gratitude to my publishing team; without them this novel would not have been possible.

CHAPTER 1

Apartheid in the Jungle

The iconic Kruger National Park in South Africa offered a diverse and intense game-viewing opportunity. As a teenager I explored its immense landscapes and spectacular wildlife with my siblings and parents. Immediately, my analytical and critical skills came into play as I focused my attention on the wildlife diversity. Like a camera lens, my eyes zoomed in on the animals in close proximity, which introduced me to an ultimately unique way to view the world. I marveled at the sight of the animals—majestic and thrilling—as the open military-green safari vehicle meandered through the wilderness. The tour guide was a tall white man with a strong Afrikaner accent who helped us explore the South African bush to experience that great safari adventure. He was neatly dressed in khaki shorts and a shirt, with a metallic green rifle hanging at his side. I immediately perceived this situation as a white man in an autocratic mode of power. The tour bus encompassed the brown and black cultures with people who were Indians, Coloureds, and a few Blacks with diverse South African accents.

My attention returned to this marvelous adventure with an abundance of wildlife in an authentic South African setting. It immediately created a visual slide in my mind, ensuring a lifetime of exotic memories, in an extravagant setting. We passed the elephants in all of their glory. These highly intelligent and delightful, huge animals herded close together, revealing their true character and personality. They enthralled us with displays of affection for their young, revealing their firm foundation as one big family. They were handsome, tall, and brown. The booming voice of the Afrikaner tour guide filled the air: "Elephants are said to be one of the most intelligent species, but sadly there are only three species left today. They need their privacy. When they migrate it is the responsibility of the eldest elephant, a male, to direct their route. They migrate in groups, and it is rare for them to travel individually."

"That's our family!" chuckled my dad as his jelly-belly jiggled with laughter.

Immediately, I drew an analogy between the situations. These elephants reminded me of the Indians who'd migrated to South Africa in a huge group, just like these elephants. I recalled how my history teacher, Mrs. Hossein, with such passion and pride had explained how the Indians had paved their way to South Africa by paying for their own passage in 1875, and they'd needed no passports because they had left British

India. Between 1860 and 1911, approximately 140,000 Indians had followed Mahatma Gandhi to South Africa. Yes, I thought he could have been the eldest elephant, a male who'd directed the route of an intelligent group of Indian settlers arriving in South Africa with their families.

My stream of thought was distracted by the Afrikaner tour guide. His voice boomed at a high pitch: "Zebras have horse-like bodies. Theoretically, the stripes help the animals withstand intense solar radiation. The black-and-white stripes are called disruptive coloration. Zebras look indistinct and may confuse predators by distorting true distance. They maintain strong family bonds."

"Much like our Coloured population," whispered my mother.

"Shh! Shh!" hushed my father.

This ultimately reminded me of our South African Coloured population. In the Afrikaans language, they were known as the Bruinmense, the brown people. They were Blacks who'd mixed with the Afrikaner and British settlers. I thought about the racial segregation laws in South Africa and how a group of people was categorized as Coloured. During the apartheid era they were neither White nor Black. They were classified as Coloureds, just like the zebras, a black-and-white mix. These interracial people had their own areas and schools due to the Afrikaner government forcing them to relocate.

My head buzzed with the voice of Mrs. Hossein: "Coloured people received an education that was inferior to Whites but superior to Blacks. The Department of Coloured Affairs was introduced in 1958. The Coloureds formed nine percent of the South African population."

Reality struck with the voice of our tour guide, Meneer Van De Merve. Initially, he introduced himself to us, by his last name.

"Daar is die springbok," he chuckled in his mother tongue, Afrikaans, a Dutch dialect, followed by English. "Sorry. The springbok is the national symbol of South Africa. Yeah, a fast animal with running speeds up to eighty to ninety kilometres an hour. They can jump up to fifteen metres. They inhabit the dry inland habitat of South Africa. Do you know that they are the largest herds of mammals in South Africa? Hunting decreased their numbers. Some perished due to the fences of farms that blocked their migratory routes. Ya, die springbok… lekker ne!" (Yeah, the springbok…nice, no?)

He ended his announcement in Afrikaans, a dialect of Dutch.

"That's South Africa's national animal," commented my father.

"That's our rugby team's mascot," added Mother.

However, my thoughts were on a deeper symbolic meaning. The springbok was South Africa's national animal. When the English and Dutch colonized South Africa in the seventeenth century, the Black tribes were the original people. I recall my history teacher telling us about the Bushmen, Hottentots, Khoikhoi, and San, the first nationals of South Africa's diversity. The Bantu-speaking people had moved into the northeastern regions hundreds of years prior to the European arrival in South Africa. Therefore, the springboks symbolized the Black population in South Africa since they were the country's original and largest group of people.

I observed the elephants, zebras, and springboks nestling side by side at the waterfront and under the trees. They instantly reminded me of the Indians, Coloured, and Blacks who formed the non-White population in South Africa. With racial segregation each group lived in its own residential area, next to each other. Nevertheless, just like these animals, they lived in peace and harmony, respecting each other's privacy. The non-White population was the majority, yet the Whites imposed minority rule upon us. The Afrikaner government segregated us by giving each group its own schools, residential areas, beaches, parks, and public services, which were inferior to those of the White people. As non-Whites, the Indians, Coloured, and Blacks shared common public facilities like washrooms, parks, transportation, and many more. We symbolized the three animals and exemplified how we could live side by side, sharing and caring for each other. Yet the White man could neither live with the non-Whites, nor could they share public places with us. They encompassed the English and Afrikaans groups and compelled us to live separately based on race.

My stream of consciousness returned to the animals of the game reserve. It was a peaceful and calm setting, with a great diversity of animals in such a complex situation. They baked under the hot African sun as insects played a game of hide-and-seek, hiding in different parts of the animals' bodies. As I sat back and tried to digest such an exotic moment, a visual slide encompassed my mind and the lyrics of "The Lion Sleeps Tonight" filled my head and moved my spirit and soul.

> *In the jungle, the mighty jungle*
> *The lion sleeps tonight*

The voice of Solomon Linda and his group echoed through my mind in that strong Zulu dialect as if it were an elaborate audition in a peaceful jungle. This was interrupted by a unique event.

With a lack of stamina, a pride of preying lions crept along the long, dried grass.

"Oh my God, look! Lions!" The words echoed through the bus like a chorus.

The thick, cumbersome mane of the lion was visible in various shades of blond. Intermittent bursts of excitement flowed through the tour bus, manifesting a conversation amongst the Indian, Coloured and Black people. Ironically, it was the pride of the non-Whites to be indulging in sporadic conversation about such a captivating scene.

The lioness crept forward like a python slithering through the grass. She lagged behind like a buffalo soldier and stalked forward as if she were trying to target her prey. A child on board yelled, "Run, run, run, a lion is going to attack!" as if signaling the other animals to be cautious.

Suddenly, a pride of lionesses encircled the herd of springboks from different directions. Like a flash of lightning, a lioness leaped into the air and powerfully attacked a springbok while the helpless herd looked on. The springbok had no chance with the lioness's jaw wrapped around its mouth and nostrils. She swiped her paw and rolled around in an attempt to strangle her victim. The other lions waited for their turn to ambush the innocent prey. With precision and complexity, the lioness rolled furiously, intending to kill her chosen prey.

I thought that this warfare went beyond food. The lions revealed their aggressive nature to the tourists. They dominated and promoted fear in the other animals. They marked their territorial boundaries, not allowing any other animal to encroach upon their land.

The lioness gave a ferocious roar, which echoed throughout the game reserve. She employed every trick of a hunter, creating a sense of panic in the other animals around. The springbok waved its hind legs like a baby kicking when it sees a colorful mobile. The lioness's sharp claws and canine teeth cut through the neck of the springbok, causing blood to ooze out as the devastating kicks of the springbok subsided. She immobilized the poor springbok and killed it instantly as we all watched helplessly. The agile springbok died with such vicious pain. The lion proved to be the most powerful animal in the jungle. Teamwork was evident when the other lions moved in for the kill.

The non-Whites on the tour bus did not react in shock. The situation was so familiar to them. My father uttered, "They are symbolic of the dominant race."

"Yes, it is the same struggle that we face each day," expressed my mother.

I knew exactly what they were talking about. My mind flashed back to the Sharpeville massacre on March 21, 1960. It had been a peaceful protest, exemplified by good discipline. I immediately drew an analogy between that situation and the springboks that peacefully grazed at the waterfront. Like the herd of springboks, seven thousand or more Blacks peacefully marched. An Afrikaner colonel drew his handgun and fired a shot, causing panic. Metaphorically, the lioness caused the same panic when she made the fierce leap to attack a springbok.

At Sharpeville, injured and bloody children lay helpless on the streets in a stream of blood. The Blacks converged at a local police station because some Blacks were arrested for not carrying their passbooks, similar to passports. Just like the lions, the mood of the White policemen turned hostile. They fired over the crowd with their submachine guns. The scuffle was tense and fierce. The victims had no power to retaliate. The situation turned bloody. The Blacks had no weapons when the devastation struck. The massacre was a personification of evil. The repression of the Blacks was entrenched in the laws of the apartheid government. It was an era of error.

"That was dramatic," laughed Mr. Van De Merve.

"Not as dramatic as the Sharpeville massacre," uttered my father with anger.

Mr. Van De Merve ignored his comment as the other non-Whites on board agreed with emotional conviction. It was as if my father read my thoughts because the images of the Sharpeville massacre went through my mind.

My mind went back to the enactment of apartheid laws in 1948. I recalled how Mrs. Hossein had drilled such facts into our heads. However, I could not help but synthesize such a situation. White dominance and racial segregation was what the South African government had had in mind. The laws of compliance were not original. I thought that it was a case of "monkey see, monkey do." The political laws were based on the laws of the jungle. The Whites were the supreme power, and they maintained full control over the whole non-White community, who feared their demeanor. The White government symbolized the lions that could pounce on their prey at any given time. They maintained political rights by denationalizing millions of South Africans. We became aliens in our own country. Thousands of Indians, Coloured, and Blacks died in custody after gruesome acts of torture by the White government. Once again, these were the laws of the jungle, where each group of animals inhabited its own land while the lions established themselves as the kings of the jungle, free to move anywhere.

To me it seemed like these animals had made an ultimate contribution to the apartheid system. They'd sparked a significant idea in the minds of the White supreme government. The laws of the lions shaped South African politics and society. This is where my view differed from the one presented to me by my history teacher, who provided us with an explicit outline of the precursors of the apartheid era.

As we exited the gates of Kruger National Park, we passed a brown brick building with a huge black-and-white sign that read UNDER SECTION 37 OF THE BYLAWS THIS WASHROOM IS RESERVED FOR THE SOLE USE OF MEMBERS OF THE WHITE RACE GROUP.

The non-White group was allotted its own washroom in an area farther away.

That day I decided to record my memorable experience in my diary.

> *Dear Diary this is my rap song,*
> *I wish you could sing along,*
> *Went on a safari this afternoon,*
> *The jungle has its own tune,*
> *Animals segregated into groups,*
> *Some sticking to their own troops,*
> *Other groups have their own herd,*
> *A group of jocks and then the nerd,*
> *This is where the apartheid era began,*
> *A bright idea picked up by the white man,*
> *The animals do not mix,*
> *An apartheid law they cannot fix,*
> *In South Africa land so great,*
> *Animals experience a segregated fate,*
> *The lions are theWhite race,*
> *Segregation is such a disgrace,*
> *They project vicious power,*
> *Controlling animals by the hour,*
> *Elephants symbolic of the Indian race,*
> *Family values is what they embrace,*
> *A firm leader maintains the bond,*
> *Their emotional ties are so fond,*

Zebras are symbolic of the Colored race,
Black and white mix is what they face,
A biracial group live on their own,
Genetic engineering or a clone,
The Springboks symbolic of a black,
Freedom of movement they lack,
South Africa is their birth land,
A pride of lions surround like a band,
Apartheid in the jungle studied by Colonist,
Picked up segregated ideas in a long list,
Dear Diary now you know where the apartheid began,
Animals gave ideas to the Dutch man,
Making them the vain antagonist,
All the non-whites the protagonist.
The superior race showed apathy,
But there were some who showed empathy.

CHAPTER 2

Apartheid Passbook

My grandmother lived in a bungalow-style house in a downtown area in the city. I loved visiting her or living with her because it was close to all the Indian shopping centres. At an early age, I developed an ardent love of shopping. English was my first language and mother tongue, since I was a fourth-generation Indian South African. I did not pick up any other Indian language, so I called my grandmother nothing but Grandmother.

Grandmother had a Black maid named Freeda. She was a young woman in her early twenties who became part of the family. Freeda lived in a room just outside the main home, called an outbuilding. However, she shared the same kitchen as Grandmother, when it came to preparing meals. Freeda was not allowed to live in the city because she was Black. She lived with her family in a homeland far away from the city. She left her homeland because she needed the money to support her family. Once I overheard a conversation between Grandmother and Freeda.

"Do you have your passbook?" asked Grandmother.

"Yes, madam, you can keep it for me," said Freeda with a strong Zulu accent.

"Do you know that Princess, the maid next door, got caught when she went to the corner shop to buy bread?" Grandma spoke softly as if the walls had ears.

"Yes, madam! Mbeki, Mrs. Naidu's maid, told me that they threw her into a small caged van with other Black men and women who were also caught in the city. She cried so much," said Freeda.

"I hope that they understand that you need money. There are no jobs in your homeland," sobbed Grandmother.

"They will be locked up in prison and tortured," said Freeda.

When I asked Grandma what they were talking about, she explained to me about the passbook. She told me that all non-Whites had to carry a passbook to identify which race group they belonged to. However, if a Black person was found in the city without a passbook, he or she was fined and imprisoned. Furthermore, Blacks were not allowed to live outside their townships or homelands. Grandma lived in an all-Indian residential area. The passbook was a symbol of oppression. Whites did not require a passbook because they were free to go anywhere. This was inherent in the apartheid system that stripped non-Whites of dignity and respect.

The passbook violated all their rights to freedom. It regulated the movement of Blacks into urban areas. My grandma explained to me how my uncle was arrested in the Orange Free State when his car broke down because Indians were not allowed in an all-White area in the Orange Free State. Uncle arrived home with a bruised eye after being tortured by a White policeman.

"As you grow up you will understand the wrath of the apartheid system," explained Grandmother.

"I pray to God that when you are older, the Whites will be defeated and all non-Whites will be free," said Freeda with a click of her tongue between each word.

Since Grandmother lived in an all-Indian area, a lot of the women wore punjabi suits and saris in a spectrum of colors and fabrics. Traditional punjabi suits were beautifully designed with traditional embroidery. The suit gained its status because it was a comfortable outfit for Indian women of all ages. It was at the top of the popularity chart as a garment suitable for many occasions. I thought it was hilarious when Grandmother bought Freeda several punjabi suits as an integral part of her day-to-day wear. Seeing a Black woman in a punjabi made me laugh.

"Is this a user-friendly garment, suitable for a maid?" I laughed.

"I reinvented this suit and combined it with creativity and talent because I need to disguise Freeda. If she is outside doing the washing, she can be caught by the White policemen and locked up," explained Grandmother.

Freeda tied the punjabi scarf around her head. As she hung the wet clothing on the line in the backyard, she resembled an Indian woman. Even Granddad was fooled when he walked in from work. Freeda could not be vilified or hunted down as a fugitive. Nevertheless, Grandmother worried about her because Freeda was heavily pregnant. On several occasions Grandmother asked her to return to her homeland on accouchement leave, but she refused to go. She wanted to continue working until the end.

On one warm summer day, I sat at the dining room table sketching in my art book, which I enjoyed very much. Grandmother was in the adjacent kitchen cooking chicken curry for lunch and mutton biryani for dinner. Grandmother enjoyed cooking and indulged in it with great pleasure. The pleasant aroma of the curried chicken wafted throughout the house, lingering in every room. The mere thought of curry for lunch excited me, as it was such an intimate part of the Indian lifestyle. To the South African Indian community, it was tastefully divine and charming because we were in love with curry. The aroma of the blend of spices wandered from room to room like a curious pet. Since it was a predominantly Indian area, the irresistible scents of aromatic spices from each home's Indian cuisine made their way through the neighbourhood. The aromas that wafted through the house activated my salivary glands, and I began to drool. It was Grandmother's culinary art at its best. The roasted masala and garam masala blends, which added a variety of flavors to the biryani, stimulated my appetite. The aromas of the spices, which are the basis of authentic Indian cooking, explored my brain. I recalled learning to eat hot, spicy Indian food long before I'd learned the letters of the alphabet.

Freeda danced around with the broom like an expert. She displayed diverse postures and expressions as she swept the hardwood floors. She engaged in every conventional standard to fluidly maneuver the broom across the floor. She moved counterclockwise around the rectangular dining room floor as if dancing to the music that played on the radio. Cleaning to Freeda was entertaining and relaxing. She knew all the components of housecleaning and mastered each one, using different methods for different areas. She had great ideas for cleaning solutions. Grandmother was a self-confessed neat freak, and Freeda made the biggest impression in the least amount of time. As she cleaned she tuned in to the broad style of popular music on the radio. Listening to music while cleaning had a psychological effect on her. It was as if it fit into her structured schedule as she sang along, knowing the words of each song.

"What are you drawing, artist?" she asked me.

"A picture of you cleaning," I laughed.

"I love it," she said with a warm smile.

Suddenly that smile turned into a deep frown, and I thought that she was upset with my drawing. There was a gush of water on the floor, which signaled to me that Freeda could not make it to the washroom in time to urinate. I laughed heartily. A colorless and odorless fluid trickled all over the hardwood floor.

"Oh dear me, you just cleaned the floors," I laughed.

"Call madam quickly!" yelled Freeda as she crouched on the floor over the liquid. She cried in pain.

"Grandmother!" I yelled. "Freeda had an accident!"

"What? Pardon me?" Grandmother came running out of the kitchen as if she knew what to expect. She immediately picked up the phone and called Aunty Thulsi, who lived down the road.

"Her amniotic sac ruptured!" Grandmother yelled. "Come immediately! She is experiencing labor contractions!"

Thulsi Aunty, as we called her, was a midwife. She performed backstreet abortions at home. She also helped a lot of Indian women with delivering their babies. I later learned that Grandmother could not rush Freeda to the hospital because she would be arrested for being in the city or in an Indian residential neighbourhood. Thulsi Aunty was there like a flash of lightning. The baby made its way down the birth canal as Freeda cried in excruciating pain. What surprised me the most was that Grandmother had always yelled at me to exit the room when she and Granddad were gossiping or if there were adults in the room. This time she did not even notice me. I ceased to exist. The excitement was all around Freeda. Thulsi Aunty was also noted for her aggressive attitude towards children. Yet she did not notice me observing the childbirth process.

Suddenly, like a dressed chicken, the baby popped out, covered in a white liquid. My heart skipped a beat and I almost jumped out of my skin as Thulsi Aunty slapped the baby with conviction. At one stage the baby resembled the receiver of a telephone, as it was attached to its mother with the umbilical cord. The baby gave a loud and lusty cry, which Thulsi Aunty eagerly anticipated.

A star was born: Freeda's baby had made a grand entrance into the apartheid era. We spectators glued our eyes on this baby boy as he made a tremendous attempt to inhale a lungful of fresh air. This led to a dramatic silence. Only music filled the air as the DJ on the radio introduced Johnny Mathis. It was such a quiet moment as the enticing voice of Johnny Mathis filled the room. Ironically, the words of the song were so apt to the situation that it made me emotional. Tears streamed down my face as I locked my eyes on this beautiful baby boy, while my mind wandered off with the voice of Johnny Mathis.

> All across the land dawns a brand new morn
> This comes to pass when a child is born

This song became my theme song for Freeda's baby boy. Ironically, the words "but a child that will grow up and turn tears to laughter, hate to love, war to peace…" are what we needed during the apartheid regime in South Africa.

Grandmother broke the silence with joy in her voice. "We can call him Fabian," she said.

"Yes, Fabian!" echoed Freeda.

"You can take him to the Department of Bantu Affairs and register him when you are well."

Grandmother was overjoyed. Freeda moved into the main house with Fabian, and Grandmother enjoyed taking care of him while Freeda recovered. Months passed by and Fabian grew into a beautiful baby boy. Fabian tugged at our heartstrings. I loved visiting Grandmother just to play with him. He could melt even the toughest heart. He made his presence felt with his laughter, cries, obnoxious diaper changes, and gurgles that gave me a feeling of ecstasy. He was irresistible and cute, with his dark mocha skin and flashing big eyes. Freeda endowed upon us such a beautiful gift. I called him my living doll. The months flew by like a jet plane. When he turned three months old, he recognized all of us with his bright smile and gurgles.

While Freeda cleaned the house, she tied Fabian on her back with a bedsheet and a towel, which was comfortable and versatile. It was almost as if he'd grown on her back. It was like his mother's movements were exercising him. He'd fall off to sleep to the beat of his mother's heart.

One day the phone rang and Grandmother picked it up. She began to panic. Aunty Pushpa notified her that the police were raiding the neighbourhood, looking for Black maids. Without hesitation Grandmother hid Freeda and Fabian in the spice pantry. She then went to the backyard and began to pray to the sun with passion and intensity. The police filtered through the Indian neighbourhood. It was a universal system that projected hatreds for Blacks. The police made pass raids at any hour of the day or night.

"Why are they coming?" I inquired.

"The pass law is designed to ensure that Blacks stay in their tribal homelands and to keep them unemployed. The creation of these homelands symbolizes the heart of the apartheid system," explained Granddad as he observed Grandmother praying to the sun as if she were yelling at God in her loud whisper. This was usual when Grandmother had a problem.

It was about noon, and there was a loud and hammering bang at the door. Granddad politely opened the door with ease and confidence. Two policemen dressed in blue air force uniforms barged in. They obnoxiously pushed past Granddad.

"Do you have any *kaffir* maids?" they yelled.

"No, we do not," said Granddad.

"Move, coolie!" retorted one, pushing Granddad aside.

I'd heard the word "kaffir" several times before. My parents referred to it as a bad word and asked us not to include it in our vocabulary because it was a derogatory word for a black South African. They called it an ethnic slur. I could feel the racial tension as the two White policemen, one with an Afrikaner accent and the other with a strong British accent, offensively made their way throughout the house. The term "coolie" was also used frequently for an Indian. It was also a racial slur and a derogatory term used during the apartheid era.

The two policemen seized control over the house and ransacked every corner. They opened every closet door. I remember distinctly how they swiped their batons under each bed, hoping to find someone. The quietness of the day was disrupted by the police presence. I was terrified because it looked like a dangerous game of hide-and-seek.

They spent a lot of time in the bedrooms. My heart beat faster as they drew closer to the kitchen area. The laws of racial segregation were tense and confusing. I felt empathy for Freeda and Fabian, who were in the forbidden neighbourhood. On this day I experienced the horror of the apartheid system, in conjunction with the pain of Freeda hiding in the spice pantry. The Afrikaner entered the spice pantry, and I glanced at Granddad, who had fish eyes, glassy and watery. I could not fight back the tears. The other policeman grumbled because he could not take the smell of Grandmother's pungent cooking.

"What do you coolies eat, gunpowder?" he complained.

"Garam masala," replied Granddad, trying to distract his attention.

The other policeman ran out of the spice pantry and gave a loud, continuous sneeze. His face was a vibrant shade of red, and he vigorously tried to wipe his nose on his sleeve to get rid of the smell of hot Indian spices. To our horror the sneeze woke up Fabian, who cried hysterically with fright and terror. The policemen propelled Freeda out of her hiding place, attacking her with their batons. It was my loss of innocence as I witnessed such an act of terror.

"No baas, no baas!" Freeda cried. She acted as if she could not speak English.

"Praat jy Afrikaans?" asked the Afrikaner. (Do you speak Afrikaans?)

As he violently pushed her around, Grandmother tried to grab the crying Fabian, but one of the officers hurled her against the wall and she lost balance, landing on the floor with Granddad at her side. Freeda's full lips trembled as if she were in a state of convulsions. Her hands shivered violently and involuntarily. She stuttered as she tried to speak. Fabian cried out hysterically as greenish-yellow mucous streamed down his nostrils. A lump appeared in my throat as if I had swallowed a golf ball. I had no control over my emotions, and I sobbed empathetically.

Freeda and Fabian were hurled into a large van with hard mesh all around. She was surrounded by other Black maids, both men and women. They frantically held onto the silver aluminum bars and looked on with intense fear. Grandmother cried, yelled, and cussed utter profanities in her Tamil dialect, cursing the policemen as they shoved Freeda and Fabian into the van. It was as if we were at a funeral, saying our final good-byes. There was no way we could contact Freeda because her homeland had no telephone landlines.

"Move it, move it, get in!" yelled the police officer as he violently propelled Freeda into the van like a milkman pushing his milk cart. The glare in Freeda's eyes was like a person being electrocuted. She gave a blank stare as the van drove off. Fabian lifted up his hand and stretched out his five fingers as if waving or bidding his final good-bye.

The South African government then implemented a policy of resettlement that had forced the Indian population to move out of their residential areas in the city. The best areas close to the city had to be designated for the White population. Thousands of Indians were forced to relocate under the Group Areas Act. The pattern of forced removal and destruction took Indians to new residential areas away from the city. I immediately knew that once my grandparents moved, Freeda would not be able to find them.

One day Granddad arrived home really upset.

"The Indian vegetable market has been burned down! Uncle Bala's stall is totally destroyed and he is so upset!" he cried.

"The Indians did not want their market moved, so I think the police burnt it down," relayed Grandmother.

"The government has a new market area in our new Indian residential area away from the city. Uncle Bala is still so sad," explained Granddad.

"What to do? We have no choice," Grandmother commented.

The Group Areas Act was implemented in full force despite resistance and protests. Grandmother stood still in her bottle-green sari, her hair freshly washed but rather thick and coarse. She was noted for being a drama queen and she bitterly tugged on her hair and began to scream and cuss, using utter profanities. She melodramatically called upon the sun and the moon, in her Indian vernacular, to stop such crisis. It was a crazy sight that brought a smirk to my sullen face.

CHAPTER 3

The End of High School

My matriculation year, which was equivalent to grade twelve, had finally come to an end. I had attended an all-girl, exclusively Indian high school. After four years at high school, I had numerous friends. The excitement of high school was sharing interesting news with my best friend, Cherry. She was slender and tall, a beautiful Indian girl who belonged to the popular group. Cherry was a drama queen, which made our years at high school even more vibrant.

I had passed my matriculation with straights As. On the last day of high school, which was a bittersweet moment, we bid our farewells to both teachers and peers. Laughter and tears filled the school. Tears flowed like a downpour of rain, yet our spirits were still elated, enthusiastic, and electric. The genuine excitement emerged from our pride of being accepted into university, which gave us mutual respect and confidence. With inspiration, intrinsic motivation, and a pinch of creativity, we were ready to explore university. The excitement led us to experiment with our crazy sides. Cherry, another friend Rona, and I called our parents to say that we were going out to celebrate the end of our school career and the beginning of a new one to come.

Cherry called her boyfriend, Danny, to pick us up from school. Danny arrived with his friends, who were already second year students at the same university. We decided to celebrate our university acceptance at the Durban beach. It was a pristine coastal stretch of the most beautiful aquamarine waters. The dramatic coastline was filled with sun worshippers soaking in every bit of the spectacular rays from the golden sun. It was also a surfing hotspot for those jocks, who showed off their fine muscles. Furious, metre-high waves extravagantly rolled in. We had great weather all year round. It was a hot afternoon in December, and swimming, surfing, and boogie boarding were at the top of our agenda.

We sat on the beautiful golden sand to soak up the solar rays. It was a stunningly beautiful sight. The sugar-white sand filtered through our toes as we strolled down closer to the water. There was a three-hundred-metre boardwalk leading down to the middle of the Indian Ocean. It was an immaculate spot for our celebration. It was our subtropical paradise, a magical sandy beach. It was an estuary that offered us a wild experience. The sparkling, golden to white sand stretched for miles in either direction. As we lay down, basking in the sun, we were unperturbed by a large sign nearby.

We were in paradise; however, racial segregation of the public premises was visible. The sign read

CITY OF DURBAN

UNDER SECTION 37 OF THE DURBAN BEACH BYLAWS. THIS BATHING AREA IS RESERVED FOR THE SOLE USE OF MEMBERS OF THE INDIAN COMMUNITY ONLY.

This apartheid sign was written in English, our first language, and Afrikaans, our second language. It was also written in Zulu, which was a common language spoken by most Blacks. The waters of the Indian Ocean mixed, yet each racial group—the Whites, Coloureds, Blacks, and Indians—had their own beach separated by a superficial fence, which looked like a shark net. Segregation, however, often allowed us to maintain close contact and bond with our own racial group. It was a special separation of races.

"Is this not ironic? We are at the Indian Ocean. Yes, Indian Ocean. Maybe under the laws of our apartheid government, we should claim this ocean ours and not let any other race group sail, surf, or swim in it!" I sarcastically chuckled.

"Hey, here's to all the *charhoes*," chuckled Cherry.

Charhoes was a slang term used to address all Indians by Indians themselves.

"Look what I have," laughed Danny.

"Lekker, man!" exclaimed his friend Neil.

Danny pulled out a bottle of cocorico, an alcoholic coconut-blend liquor.

"Come on, Kay, you have to try some," Cherry excitedly urged me on.

"I'll try some," said Rona.

"That's my girl, Rona," said Cherry with vigor and enthusiasm.

"I have not tried alcohol before. I do not think that I'm going to like it," I squealed in an innocent chipmunk-like tone.

"Let's get it *on*!" exclaimed Cherry.

I thought about my ability to think rationally being impaired. I was just seventeen. I did not know what to expect when I got to know the secret realm of alcohol for the first time. Cherry swallowed her first glass down like a glutton.

"Hey, Kay, stop being a party pooper. Remember, we are here to celebrate!" yelled Cherry.

"It's not that bad," slurred Rona after a few sips from her glass.

I forged ahead, fighting my own toughest antialcohol laws. Ironically, these personal laws seemed tougher than the apartheid laws. I took my first sip with the group cheering. It was important for me to drink responsibly and stay within my alcohol tolerance level, my ability to maintain self-control. We had a respectable establishment of friends, which was of vital importance. We were a close-knit group of boys and girls who hung out as a clique. There was no potential of our drinks being spiked. I hated the taste of the alcohol in cocorico, but I loved the lingering taste of coconut in my mouth. I realized that I did have the unique ability to tolerate alcohol. It was time to enjoy the company, celebrate, and feel free. Ram and Rona adopted a steady and slow pace as they sipped their drinks and enjoyed the music playing on the small cassette player with a booming sound. We all got up and danced to the rhythm of Bob Marley's "No Woman, No Cry," which filled the air on our sacred spot on the beach. The song took over our hearts and souls as we swayed to its beat.

No woman no cry

The song continued at full blast as we moved to its beat. A White jogger passing the Indian beach yelled, "Calm down, coolies!"

We did not protest but continued to sing along to Bob Marley, giving the jogger the finger.

> *Everything's gonna be all right*
> *Forget your past...*

Ironically, this was our way of reassuring ourselves that this apartheid system that we lived in wouldn't get us down and that everything would be all right, so there was no need to shed any tears. Bob Marley's powerful words gave us some reassurance of a better future, when the laws of the apartheid system would be dismantled.

At this stage the alcohol had consumed Cherry instead of Cherry consuming the alcohol. She was beginning to get drunk, which placed her in a funnier and happier spirit.

"I am hungry, *ek se*!" yelled Cherry in slang typically used by South African Indians.

"What do you want to eat?" asked Danny.

"How about bunny chow?" we all exclaimed in a chorus.

I loved bunny chow. It was an Indian South African fast-food dish sold at the Durban beach. A loaf of bread was hollowed out and filled with curry. This unique fast food originated amongst the Durban Indian community. A myth states that during the apartheid era in South Africa, Indians were not allowed in some shops and restaurants. Therefore, shop owners illegally served Indians through back windows of their shops. An efficient and quick way to serve them was to cut out the middle portion of a loaf of white bread and fill it with chicken or mutton curry. They then capped the filling with the portion of bread that was dug out. It came in quarter, half, or full loaves.

We sat around the loaf of mutton bunny chow, attacking it with our fingers. The gravy of the mutton curry soaked into the walls of the bread. Sharing one bunny chow amongst six of us was outrageous. The fusion of spices added to the flavor, and the aroma filled the air. The mix of masala, curry powder, ginger, garlic, and tomato stimulated our taste buds. The crust formed the delicious bowl. We dipped into the curry with the scooped out centre and tucked in. It was food that defined the South African Durban Indians. It was a messy finger affair with utensils out of the picture. It was love at first bite.

Cherry exclaimed, "That was lekker!"

"Finger-licking good," replied Danny.

"What would we do without our Indian cuisine?" uttered Rona.

"Charhoes are the best!" exclaimed Neil.

We just laughed and spoke utter nonsense. The boys took a refreshing swim as the girls admired the magnificent view. The lagoon was a picture-perfect sight. The large waves crashed on the shore, causing a foamy, white-lather effect. The boys rocked the waves, diving into each crescent formation and riding it to shore. It was our Indian paradise in our quaint little spot on the beach. The huge waves rose and splashed down like humpback whales.

"My bladder is bursting," I said

"Me too," said Cherry.

We walked to the washroom. There was a sign that read

NON-WHITES

NIE-BLANKES

The sign was to remind us that the washrooms were for non-Whites only, another enforcement of the devious policy of the apartheid regime. When I travelled to other countries, the washroom signs differentiated between sexes, stating male or female. However, these most bizarre and humiliating signs divided Whites from non-Whites, as if we were denied the citizenship rights to enter any washroom or restroom. Heightened security was present to see that non-Whites did not break the rules. Petty apartheid laws regulated our everyday segregated lifestyle. The non-Whites washrooms were in a bad state. We got out of there as fast as possible.

We continued to party on the beach with music, food, drinks, and good company, oblivious to the apartheid signs. Those symbolic signs could not dampen our spirits. We stuck to our social policy of having fun in the comfort of our own group of people.

"It's time to go home," said Danny.

Cherry was the only one who was intoxicated.

"The atmosphere around me is getting aggressive, I guess I must be drunk," she slurred incoherently. "No, I see the world spinning right in front of…my…eyes," she laughed.

We got into the car and drove off. Cherry insisted on sticking her feet out the window because her toes needed fresh air. Alcohol was a legitimate excuse for such behaviour. She kept us entertained with her slurred speech and impaired balance. Her loss of muscle coordination made her flop around like a rag doll, with her toes still stuck out of the car window.

We passed the Golden Mile, which was a fantastic stretch of beachfront near the central business district and the tourist attractions. The architecture was simply spectacular and featured popular nightclubs and restaurants. We passed Mini Town with its miniature replicas of the best of Durban. The snake park was next to that with a massive collection of a variety of reptiles. The marine world and water park were breathtaking to view. However, the Golden Mile was designated a predominantly White area, which we could not participate in. Traditional market vendors sat on the streets selling their intricate Zulu arts and crafts, and the massive pleasure parks—with their swimming and splash pools, water fountains, waterslides, fun fairs, and curio markets—were a spectacular sight for passengers of cars driving by.

A colorfully dressed Zulu man with elaborate headgear pulled a rickshaw, running, hopping, skipping, and jumping. An elderly White couple sat on a seat at the back as he pulled them along, singing in Zulu. His spectacular beads and sequins glittered in the hot Durban sun. He entertained his guests at a small price. It was a sight that etched a long-lasting, beautiful memory in my mind.

"Say good-bye to such a beautiful sight as we head home," warned Danny.

We turned north and headed for the Indian residential areas where we lived, away from the city centre. The white residential areas surrounded the central business district. The Whites had the residential areas along the coastline with the highest property values. They surrounded the periphery of the city. The apartheid regime had a profound influence on the social, physical, and economic landscape of the country.

The driving around had sobered Cherry a little. She could not remember all her dramatic antics. She was just happy to be together with her friends, whom she loved dearly. I believed that the bread from the bunny chow had filled her stomach and absorbed the alcohol.

"Nobody makes me feel the way cocorico does!" giggled Cherry.

"You were smashed," laughed Rona.

"Poking fun at the level of my intoxication?" Cherry giggled.

"You had fun!" exclaimed Neil.

"I remember going into that non-White washroom and sitting on the toilet. Then, every time I tried to flush, something came up and squeezed my butt. Finally, I realized that I was sitting on the mop bucket and not the toilet seat," laughed Cherry.

Our laughter was contagious as we burst into a hysterical fit of uncontrollable giggles.

CHAPTER 4

Ethnic University

The university I attended was no different from high school because it was also all Indian. There were some Coloureds and Blacks, but too few to notice. It was established for the Indian population during the apartheid era. Registration date was on January 1, and the academic year ended in December. The first few months were simply fantastic because they spelled out freedom. We had a lot of time to socialize with friends while lending time to our academic needs. We attended a lot of social gatherings. Lectures were amazing because we were with friends we knew. At times we studied in groups at the library, which made studying smooth sailing. Our favourite spot was the cafeteria, where we gathered in a large group of boys and girls to eat and chat. Cherry and I took the same courses in the arts department, so we continued to bond and strengthen our friendship. Her boyfriend, Danny, was in the science department, so he met up with us during his breaks.

About five blissful months passed by, and then the situation at university grew tense. Students staged a boycott of lectures, as ordered by the student council. Nelson Mandela had been imprisoned and tortured for several years on Robben Island. He was our heroic figure. Several Indian professionals had also been arrested and locked up as political prisoners. Their main objective was to abolish the apartheid system and bring about a nation that was free socially, politically, and economically. The situation at university deteriorated and widespread intimidation increased. The student council called for a political assembly to be held in the huge auditorium. One of the main items on the agenda was the discussion of the legal system of political and social separation of all four races in South Africa, namely Whites, Blacks, Indians, and Coloureds. It was a system implemented by the apartheid regime. There were many passionate and outspoken Indian students who wholeheartedly expressed their intolerance for White supremacy. I grew increasingly anxious to listen to various political speakers who saw political change as inevitable.

"Rumor has it that we are going to have powerful political speakers today," said Cherry.

"That would be amazing," replied Danny.

"A few of our students were arrested and locked up at another political rally held outside campus," Neil informed us.

"That adds fuel to the fire," commented Danny.

A member of the student representative council welcomed us and introduced the next speaker, a famous Indian lawyer known for being a political activist. His speech was dynamic, animated, vibrant, and passionate. His voice echoed through the auditorium like thunder. The crowd was as silent as the night.

"We live in the most beautiful country in the world. Yet we long for an egalitarian society free of discrimination, where all races—Whites, Blacks, Indians, and Coloureds—could live as one united nation. Each one present today has to dedicate himself or herself to fight for the elimination of racial segregation in South Africa. You have to be a visible advocate for the freedom and rights of all our people. Racial discrimination harms us like a dagger through our backs. It brings out the inherent differences in people's traits. Our extremist government breeds hatred, exploitation, separatism, racial supremacy, and vigilantism. Let's fight against such genocide in South Africa. Let's unite all races, ethnic groups, cultures, and people as one South African nation. Amandla!"

"Awethu!" chanted the crowd.

"Amandla!" chanted the lawyer.

"Awethu!" responded the crowd.

The chanting continued with passion and animation. It was Zulu terminology for "power to the people," words that spelled out our struggles against oppression. The louder we chanted, the more we demonstrated our resistance against the apartheid regime. We wanted our apartheid White government to hear our cries and address our grievances.

"Ngawethu! Amandla! Ngawethu! Amandla! Ngwethu! Amandla! Ngawethu! Power to the poor people!" cried a group of people from the back of the auditorium.

The crowd responded with the shedding of tears, sobbing, sniffling, weeping, whimpering, and bawling. Emotion swept through the crowd as each speaker delivered an emotional speech. The apartheid system inflicted pain too complex to verbalize;

this was our way of dealing with the apartheid situation. The rally reinforced our determination to get rid of apartheid.

"Do you have a tissue?" asked Cherry.

"I'll need one too!" cried Neil.

This was followed by the heart-throbbing singing of anti-apartheid songs, which moved the crowd that suffered under the torturous acts of apartheid policies. The words of "Nkosi Sikelel' iAfrika," "Lord Bless Africa" in the Xhosa language, filled the auditorium. This song replaced the Afrikaans national anthem, "Die Stem van Suid-Afrika." It obviously was an act of political defiance to rebel against the South African apartheid government. We sang with emotion, empathy, and pathos.

> *God bless Africa*
> *Raise high its glory*
> *Hear our prayers*
> *God bless us, her children*
> *God, we ask you to protect our nation*
> *Intervene and end all conflicts*
> *Protect us, protect our nation,*
> *Our nation, South Africa*
> *South Africa*
>
> *From the blue of our heaven*
> *From the depth of our sea*
> *Over our everlasting mountains*
> *Where the echoing cliffs resound*
> *Sounds the call to come together*
> *And united we shall stand*
> *Let us live and strive for freedom*
> *In South Africa, our land.*
> *Nkosi sikelel' iAfrica*
> *Maluphakanyisw' uphondo lwayo...*

This song was sung in Xhosa, Zulu, Sotho, Afrikaans, and English. A black activist who took the microphone and stunned the crowd with her dynamic voice led this song. We could hear every click of her tongue and the beat of the drum in her voice. As we sang along with her, our hearts were filled with a clear vision of a freed and prosperous South Africa. This song energized us. I could visualize a South Africa filled with peace and harmony. Our vibrant voices filled the auditorium, and we sang as if the apartheid government could hear it. We sang to heal South Africa of the cancerous disease called apartheid.

As I sang along with passion and dedication, I thought about my past and present in South Africa. I am a fourth-generation South African. My great-grandparents arrived in South Africa from India as businesspeople. My grandparents and parents were born in South Africa. I did not visit India. The only culture that I was familiar with was the South African culture. This included its traditions and upbringings. Therefore, South Africa was my country and place of birth. It was my land of hope and joy. This was why I wanted to see positive change.

The student representative announced that we could take a break. Emotions still ran high as we progressed to the area in front of the auditorium and cafeteria. It was a beautiful sight. The weather was marvelous, the radiant South African sun shining down upon us as if promising a brighter future. There was a pond in the opposite area with elegant and beautiful white ducks floating around. A ramp gracefully wound its way up to the library. The campus reminded me of St. Marco Square in Venice with all its splendor and beauty.

The main entrance of the university was also an exotic sight. A troop of vervet monkeys, in bright shades of grey with black faces and white fringes, played together. They socialized in a group of twenty, with one dominant male. The babies clung to their mothers, as if suffering from separation anxiety. They patiently waited for pieces of bread given to them by students. The bushes around the university were the monkeys' natural habitat, where they fed on highly fragmented vegetation.

Cherry, Danny, Neil, Rona, Ram, and I sat on a cemented area to eat lunch. We enjoyed a jointly contributed meal, a peer-oriented picnic. We all opened our lunches to share, which was so intimate. The six of us shared our deli sandwiches and finger foods.

"Try my chicken roti sandwich," said Cherry.

"I cannot resist that!" replied Danny.

"You blatantly refuse to share your secret recipe," giggled Rona.

"I have a deep-seated love for your chicken roti," I commented.

Our picnic meal was fragrant, spicy, colorful, and simple. The fine combination of potatoes, chicken, and tomato sauce wrapped inside the roti pancakes was delicious and flavourful, a highly addictive food for any Indian person. As we ate, a member of our student representative council walked around with his loud hailer, also known as a bullhorn, singing "Nkosi Sikelel' iAfrika." The bullhorn amplified his voice throughout the campus. His melodious tone spread evenly in every direction.

Suddenly, the students began running, panicked. The peaceful atmosphere turned into a state of turmoil. The South African police and riot squad, with opaque riot shields and protective helmets, took charge. Even the troop of monkeys dispersed in fear. The police were armed with nonlethal weapons, like batons and whips. They used a long-range acoustic device to announce their grand entrance.

"Run, run, run!" yelled Danny at the top of his lungs.

"Oh my God, help us!" cried Cherry.

"Stay close to me, Cherry! Let's not lose each other!" I sobbed, running in heels.

The crowd of students moved in different directions. Cherry and I lost Rona, Ram, Neil, and Danny in the crowd. We ran into the building that read SCIENCE FACULTY. Just to the left, at the entrance of the building, Cherry and I found the ladies' washroom. We ran into it and locked ourselves in a toilet stall. At this stage we were in tears. I shook as if I were having a fit of epilepsy. Cherry fell on the toilet floor; she held her stomach and cried hysterically. Loud, terrified screams came from outside, which made me cringe. The toilet stalls were made of solid red brick. Higher up on the wall, I spotted several parallel openings in the brick, which served as vents, allowing air to enter.

"What's going on outside?" asked Cherry.

"I have the same question on my mind," I replied.

"Sounds scary," whimpered Cherry.

"I'm going to check," I replied with a shaky voice.

I held onto the wall beside the toilet. I placed my left foot onto the closed toilet bowl. Carefully, I lifted my right foot and stood firmly. I balanced myself with both hands on the wall and looked through the vertical brick vents. The parallel gaps were about three to four inches wide. My body trembled at what I saw. The vents on the wall were like a camera lens to the outside world. Although a lot of students had run away in fear from the riot police, masses of students bravely stayed behind to try to negotiate with the riot squad.

The sight was scary. There were lots of students lying on the ground because the police had beaten them. Red seemed to be the predominant color of the concrete as blood oozed out of their open wounds. The riot squad was vicious. They looked like laborers in a sugar cane field. They worked their batons like sickles, the curved blades used for harvesting grain crops.

Students screamed in pain as the batons lashed against their bodies.

"Help, help! Stop, stop!" cried a pregnant student.

"Stop! She is pregnant!" yelled another.

"My baby, oh my God, my baby!" cried the pregnant student.

"What's going on, Kay?" asked Cherry.

"Oh my God, Cherry! Oh...my...God!"

Cherry climbed up onto the toilet pan and placed both hands upon my shoulders for support and balance. The lid of the toilet bowl dented, and we thought that we were going to fall. We struggled to maintain our balance. It was like we were watching a horror movie. Amongst the riot squad were white men dressed in casual clothing who used whips to disperse the crowd. I did not perceive any level of threat from the students, who had no weapons, not even bricks or stones. A white man furiously slashed his sjambok, an African whip made of heavy black leather, through the air.

"The one with the sjambok is a white lecturer at our university!" cried Cherry.

"Yes, I once saw him going into the staff cafeteria!" I nervously yelled.

"That bloody [*bleep, bleep*] is joining the riot squad against our Indian students!" cried Cherry as she uttered profanities.

"[*Bleep. bleep*] fool!" I cussed as all the worst profanities slid out of my mouth like bullets fired from a gun. The political views of some of the white lecturers were publicly revealed on that eventful day. All the students could do was hurl words like weapons.

More armored police vehicles pulled up at the front entrance. Hundreds of riot squad officers, with their protective helmets and riot shields, advanced towards the crowd.

They wore gas masks, which foreshadowed more danger. Some brought their police dogs. The students' mobility was restricted. They were vulnerable victims with no hope. Without warning, the riot control agents dispersed tear gas into the crowd. I watched in horror as a canister of tear gas hit the vent I was peering through and burst like a cannonball. My sight was impaired and I fell to the ground. Cherry fell over me.

The chemical produced a sensory irritation. It was as if my face had been pushed into a container of hot green chilies. My mind sped back to when my grandmother used to grind spicy, pungent, hot green chilies for the biryani she cooked. I recalled how the smell rapidly spread throughout the house, which caused my eyes to tear and made me feel as if I were suffocating. However, the tear gas was ten times worse. I immediately vomited on the floor. Cherry used the water from the toilet bowl to rinse her eyes. I could not imagine how those in close proximity to the gas felt. The mucous membranes of my eyes, mouth, and lungs were irritated. I found it hard to breathe. I could not stop crying and sneezing. I felt as if I were in a chemical warfare zone.

"We have to get out of here!" cried Cherry.

"Hold my hand and let's run!" I cried.

"Let's not lose each other," Cherry whined.

"Oh no, no, no!" I stuttered.

We left the toilet cubicle and peeped out the doors.

"Is the coast clear?" I asked.

"Just a few students running," replied Cherry.

We were still in the science building. Just outside the washroom was a telephone booth. I took out a quarter from my purse, my hands trembling.

"What are you doing?" yelled Cherry.

"I am going to call my mom!" I cried.

"No, let's get out of here before the riot police come in!" she cried hysterically.

I could not miss the chance of making a phone call. I dialed my mother's office, my fingers nervously going through the rotary dial. Cherry ran for her life, and I was left alone. My mother's secretary picked up the phone. I yelled at her to put my mother on the line.

"Why, what's the matter?" she nosily inquired.

"This is no time to be a gossipy *gangama*," I yelled at her insultingly.(a slang Indian terminology)

She immediately put my mother on the phone, and I summarized the incident to her in one huge breath.

"Pick me up immediately! My situation is going from bad to worse!" I cried hysterically.

"Where about on campus are you?" she nervously asked.

"I am…aaaah, help…no, no!" I screamed.

A tear gas canister landed on my toe, splitting the nail. I instinctively knew that the riot squad was progressing towards the science building. My heart pounded faster, and I almost jumped out of my skin. The sight of the riot squad police officers scared me. It was a situation of fight or flight, and I chose the latter. Without hesitation I dropped the telephone receiver and ran for my life. I was wearing my glass slippers,(clear plastic) with a three-inch-high heel, which was in high fashion. However, I had no time to think about how delicate my shoes were. I could feel the low vapour-pressure of the tear gas, which caused me to run faster. I ascended the wide staircase as fast as my legs could carry me. As I ran I could feel the intensive air exchange on the second floor. I left behind the toxic gas that stirred into the air on the ground floor. I looked through the huge glass window adjacent to the staircase and saw the fully armored riot control officers continuing to subdue the crowd. Other mobile officers made arrests, which didn't seem necessary. Most of the police officers had infiltrated the crowd. Other riot squad officers walked in a parallel line extending from east to west.

At this stage I was all alone. I trembled with fear, with no friends around. To add to my terror, the riot officers were noisy as they marched simultaneously. What scared me the most was the sound as they beat their shields with their batons. It evoked intense fear and psychological trauma in me. I felt unstable as a panic attack set in. I felt an overwhelming feeling of anxiety, as if I were going crazy and losing control of my sanity. Frantic agitation took control over my body.

Other frenzied students sat on the stairs. One female was subdued by another student because she wanted to jump to her death. Suicide was not an option in such a fragile situation. It seemed like my panic attack was infectious, as it spread to other vulnerable students I ran past. Groups of intelligent students became irrational as they lost control of reasoning and logical thinking. The neocortex of my brain, associated with reasoning, played games with me. At times I had no cognitive ability to reason. A group of students, like a herd of cattle, trampled into the building, forming congestion. It was fight or flight. It was the riot squad that had activated such stress. I wished I could change colour to camouflage myself, to escape being captured and tortured. The pain of being away from my close friends inflicted real psychological damage in me. My lips quivered and my body shook as I tried to flee from this potentially threatening environment. I knew that I was going to be captured and tortured. Death presented itself to me in an unfriendly and obnoxious manner. This was the end.

The noise of the batons beating violently against the shields grew louder and louder. I affiliated with other strange students, who shared the same social response to the threat. I felt my body halt and slow down. I knew that I was in the face of death. Death…death…death!

"Come on, you can do it! Give me your hand and I will help you up. Don't give up. Don't cry," said a male student who urged me to run up the stairs with him. The violent beating of the batons seemed to echo through the corridors and bounce off the walls. I felt a catastrophic sense of the walls around the staircase closing in upon me. I squeezed tightly on the hand of the stranger who helped me run up the longest flight of stairs I had ever been on. I felt the adrenaline rush, which increased my strength to move forward.

In the heat of the moment, the heel of my glass slipper cracked, triggering an increase in my heart rate and breathing. However, my intuition urged me to escape from such a combative situation. I felt a numbing sensation in my feet, and I was unaware of the severity of the crack on my toenail as blood oozed out. Just like many students around me, I was dazed. Death was the antagonist, yet he befriended us.

I spotted a large, ornate door of dark brown hardwood. It was so traditional in a contemporary world. This antique, salvaged door with stained glass and wrought-iron pieces high above was a mystery I had to explore. I felt as if I were in the medieval times, escaping into a castle through this overblown rustic door. I held onto the huge, vintage iron handle, a black-smith's masterpiece, and pulled. I wondered if heaven were beyond. I realized that behind the mystic door was my comfort zone. It was a large lecture theatre with a capacity for hundreds of students. The floors were pitched. The rear seats were much higher than the front. It looked like a Shakespearean theatre, with its efficacious design. There were desks and benches in circular format with a single focus point on the lecturer. There was a microphone and other audiovisual equipment. It was a unique lecture hall with a seating arrangement to inspire students to participate in their graduate studies. The beauty of the room brought back my senses of sight, sound, and touch.

Silence filled the air. Then I heard a few whispers. One by one, like tortoises emerging from their shells, the heads of students began to appear. I realized that when I'd opened the huge doors, they'd thought that it was a member of the riot squad and withdrew under the desks. My spirit was elevated and my imagination excited as hundreds of heads popped up. One young woman waved her hands hysterically as if doing a rave dance.

"Hey, Kay, come up here quickly!" exclaimed Cherry.

"Oh my God, dear me—it is really you?" I exclaimed in excitement.

I ran to her and hugged her with tears of joy. To add to the surprise, Neil's head popped out from under the lecturer's table at the focus point. He then spoke to us through the microphone with a whisper. That was definitely a loud whisper, and I laughed at the oxymoron.

"Let's pretend as if we are having a chemistry lecture. So if the riot squad enters, they will think that there is a lecture going on," he nervously uttered.

He tried to create and promote proactive participation by students, but we were too tense for interactions. I spotted Danny and Rona a few seats from Cherry. We exchanged glances, and the warm smiles on our faces were of comfort and support. I was pleased to know that my family of friends was close by. There were lots of other students I recognized who also brought comfort to me. Ram, Joel, Baboo, Anwar, Melanie, Rudy, and Jenny lined the front row. A student next to me bravely hummed the tune to the Beach Boys song "Student

Demonstration Time." As he hummed, the lyrics of the song took over my mind and my world. The words strengthened my soul as a visual flashed in my memory of students being beaten up by the South African riot squad. I imagined all of us in hiding, singing in a chorus after the Beach Boys.

> *Four martyrs earned a new degree*
> *The bachelor of bullets*

I could hear the sirens in the song as the Beach Boys' lyrics took over my mind. The chorus overpowered my spirit, as if an act of consolation. The voices of the Beach Boys in "Students Demonstration Time" transformed my panic attack into calmness through the system of thinking. It balanced my heart and mind. It implemented an innovative solution to my immediate crisis. It transformed my emotional, physical, cognitive, social, aesthetic, spiritual, and psychological frame into perfect health. It was therapeutic in helping me cope with such a dreadful situation. It relaxed my mind, body, and soul as I sat at the lecture desk with so many panic-stricken students. It was rhythmic entertainment that took my mind off the riot squad. The influence of the Beach Boys' song on my functional ability and behavioural mode was phenomenal. The chorus of the song played repeatedly in my mind, and I felt time slow down. It gave me a sense of independence and individuality, which helped me gain a sense of identity. It was a creative outlet to release my fear, and I was ready for self-discipline. My self-esteem grew as I turned around and saw the student next to me still humming the tune. He glanced at me and smiled. He was White, as pale as White could be. He was one of very few White students, amongst all the Brown and a few Black students. Music was a unifying force that brought different race groups together. I gave him a shy grin.

"Do you like the Beach Boys?" he asked with a warm smile.

It was not a question that I was expecting in such an emotional crisis.

"Yes, 'California Girls'…my favourite…mmm," I stuttered.

"Mine too," he replied.

"But you are White!" I uttered without thinking.

"As you can see, yes!" he sarcastically replied.

"I mean——"

He completed my sentence. "What is a White boy doing amongst all these Brown students in such a politically tense situation?"

"Yes, why are you here and hiding too?" I chuckled.

"My dad is a lawyer, and I am a law student at this university. My family believes in equal power and rights for all races. We are political activists," he seriously acknowledged. "I was also tortured by the police for helping other Black activist hide at our home. But the struggle continues," he added.

His sparkling blue eyes were so dominant, yet it is such a recessive trait. It was a variation of shades of blue, as blue as the ocean. When I looked into his blue eyes, I felt seasick. His eye colour was an inherited trait, influenced by more than one Afrikaner gene. He lacked melanin in his skin; he was so pale, with flushed cheeks. His golden blond hair framed his handsome face. I felt a little uncomfortable because it was the first time that I'd sat so close to a White male. It was a ghost encounter to me, and I felt the chills.

"You look so shocked to see me, yet I was the one who held your hand while you were struggling up those stairs," he said in a polite tone.

"Really, my body was invaded by a panic attack. I did not notice your skin colour," I giggled.

"I have your broken glass heel in my pocket," he said as he pulled out the heel to my shoe.

"I did not even realize my heel was out. All I remembered was that it had cracked," I giggled in an embarrassed tone.

I smirked as thoughts flashed in my mind. The thought of my favourite childhood fairy tale, Cinderella, brought back sweet memories. Was this my prince with my glass heel? I tried to erase such thoughts from my mind, as it was against the moral code of conduct in the apartheid era. Mixed-race dating was taboo.

I looked to my right. Cherry's head was on the desk and I knew that she was crying. That is how she reacted when a situation was critical. I rubbed her back and consoled her, telling her that we were going to be all right. Danny made his way towards her. He gave me a nasty stare as if to say, "What are you doing talking to that strange White male?" It was such a paradox, because we were in that situation demonstrating against the apartheid system. We wanted a free South Africa, free of all racial segregation, yet talking to a White seemed obnoxious to Danny. I believed that was our South African mentality. We grew up believing that the Whites were the supreme power and that non-Whites were treated with no dignity and respect. However, there was a group of professional Whites that wanted to see a free South Africa, free of all racial evil. The White colonist formed the basis for racial segregation and was responsible for the emancipation of slaves. They did not support racial egalitarianism. People like Nelson Mandela bravely fought against such evil forces of racism.

The turbulent sounds and chanting of the riot squad grew louder and louder. There was no violence in the lecture theatre to quell. It was a sign of threat and intimidation. They were White policemen who loath to see changes, and this was their strategy to implement racial discrimination. I had no time to scrutinize the situation as someone yelled, "Hide, hide! They will think that there is a political rally going on in this lecture hall!" It sounded like Neil, but in a time of intense fear, everyone's voices sound the same. Like turtles we withdrew into our shells and crouched under the lecture desks. The policemen were violating our basic human rights. We had no self-defense against such tactical weapons, training, and drills. We spread out hopelessly on the floor, trying to conceal every inch of our bodies. It was almost like a child's parody of a game of hide-and-seek.

Outside the room it sounded like a disaster zone. I heard the chanting of the riot squad and students' gut-wrenching screams. The shotguns fired rubber bullets, which bounced off the windows and walls, creating a loud din. It sounded like total pandemonium. My sense of hearing was evoked, since I could not use my sense of sight. I heard the tear gas grenades being dispensed. The sound of escalating violence was close. There was wild confusion, chaos, and uproar. The demons were closing in on us. Instantly, my life felt like a grotesque pandemonium and I wished that I were dead. Fear was intoxicating. I instantly felt the fear of a bloody confrontation with the riot police.

There was a loud thud on the door. "Silence!" yelled someone in a loud whisper. Somebody kicked open the door with excessive force. I was consumed with fear of being caught. An irrational phobia took over my body. I curled up like a fetus. My hands were like an umbilical cord holding on to Cherry. She faced borderline paralysis as she curled up into a ball. We were captive to our fears. I was agitated by the thought of death, which this devastation created. I knew that I had to surrender meekly in the hands of death. Everything seemed momentary. The sound of the riot squad was insane and antagonistic. They used a sound weapon in the lecture room as we lay harmless on the floor. I glimpsed through the separation of the chairs. Like gorillas they hopped onto every possible object at the front of the hall. Nobody was visible because the wooden coverings of the desk, which extended to the floor, concealed us. The sound cloud that hung over our heads deafened us.

Bang, bang, bang, bang! Their batons hit the surface of the desk in front. They used a long-range acoustic device to notify us of their presence, which was so ironic as their presence was felt in every dimension. I held my breath to prevent the "hic" sound from my hiccups. I could feel a full body tremor. I wondered if we would be buried alive in a mass grave. I worried about the release of tear gas. The riot squad vacated the room with no incident, and I could hear a sigh of relief from the students.

After thirty minutes there was a buzz on campus that the riot squad had left. We crawled out of our hiding places like scared rodents. There was no riot squad on the campus square, just terrified, panic-stricken students. A lot of parents arrived to pick up their children. Generosity was in the air as worried parents urged any student, not just their own, to jump into their cars in an attempt to vacate the premises promptly. Some parents made several trips back and forth to help stranded students get out of the university boom gates. Cherry, Rona, and I jumped into a red Mercedes-Benz, and the empathic driver drove us out of the main campus and onto the highway ramp. He left us there and returned to pick up more students. On the ramp Cherry, Rona and I hitchhiked a ride to Cherry's house. Lots of commuters were aware of the situation from family, friends, or the radio stations. I later discovered that my mom hastily drove to the university to pick me up, but panic-stricken students just jumped into her car and begged her to take them out of the vicinity. She was one of the parents who transported students out. She was worried, hoping to see me in the crowd, but to no avail.

CHAPTER 5

Petty Apartheid

Due to the riots at the university, it had closed down for several months, leaving the students devastated. I was a first-year student who was enthusiastic about attending lectures. A lot of Indian girls were "gold diggers," looking for rich doctors or medical school students to secure their financial future. A lot of Indian parents were also in search of doctors to secure their daughters' futures, earning the name of "gold diggers" as well. However, I was a "goal digger." I set myself positive academic goals and I intended to achieve them. My financial future depended on my intellectual and academic goals. Therefore,

I was disappointed that my goals could not be accomplished faster due to the university closure. This left me with a lot of leisure time. As a teenager, leisure time meant having fun with friends.

We lived in an elite Indian residential area that was part of a system of racial segregation enforced by the apartheid government in South Africa, ruled by the National Party. The apartheid legislation classified all Indians as Asians. Therefore, we were forced to live in an Asian neighbourhood. Residential areas were segregated into Black, White, Coloured, and Asians. Ironically, imperial and colonial powers had brought in the social class system. Indians were divided into the upper class, middle class, and lower class. Subsequently, each class lived in its own neighbourhood or residential area as well. Hence, segregation amongst the Indian community was just as trivial.

We lived in an affluent Indian neighbourhood with many upper-class families. Most Indians purchased land and built unique mansions of exquisite architecture. These houses, in all their glory, maintained the highest pricing per square foot. The upscale neighbourhood housed the elite, upper-class Indians. The social gulf between the upper-, middle-, and lower-class Indians persisted. The grandest mansions peered down on the beautiful vegetation of the forestry. Huge purple-flowered trees lined the winding roads. Indians with social and economic aspirations lived within the golden boundaries. This wealthy suburb featured the highest-rated school system with beautiful, brick-built schools stationed away from the street in a park-like setting.

The adjacent area was an upper middle-class Coloured residential area. It formed a residential fringe around the Indian area. These homes were charming, with beautiful design aesthetics and attractive architectural features. The neighbourhood included well-maintained bungalows and beautifully remodeled homes.

The Coloured residential area was sandwiched between the Indian and White neighbourhoods. The architecture of the upper-class White neighbourhood was stunning. The upscale homes were beautiful. The landscape was exotic. There was a wide array of huge houses in a heavily wooded and traditional landscape. The amazing White residential area overlooked the sparkling waters of the Indian Ocean.

I had become close friends with a few Coloured girls from the adjacent neighbourhood. Coloured girls were so different from Indian girls. They were free-spirited, carefree, and fun-loving. Socially, they lived life to the fullest. Indian girls were more timid, conservative, traditional, and passive. The Coloured girls were courageous, outspoken, and extroverts. In a situation of fight or flight, they bravely faced fear in the eye. They were sarcastic and witty, which made me enjoy their company. My close friend Ally was tall and big-boned. She was light-skinned with brown wavy hair. She had more Black features than White features. Nevertheless, she was attractive. She spoke with a strong Coloured accent. Iris was another friend. She had bright, sparkling green eyes, with dusty blond hair. Although she was Coloured, she looked White. Only a South African could tell the difference. She looked like a Barbie doll. The Coloureds who lived in Durban were different from those in Cape Town or Johannesburg. They had different accents. Then there was Lilly, who looked Indian although she was Coloured. She had a more tanned skin, with dark hair and dark eyes. She was a brown version of a Barbie doll. We often took long walks around the Indian and Coloured neighbourhoods. We were all seventeen, and despite our different races, we shared the same teenage hormones. Ally, Iris, and Lilly met me at my home.

"Let's go for a long and exciting walk," said Ally.

"Where to?" I asked.

"How about the park close to the beach?" suggested Iris as her green eyes sparkled with joy.

"Sounds good!" exclaimed Lilly.

The park was really far. We had to pass the Indian, Coloured, and White residential areas to get there. The city of Durban had exotic weather, with summer year round. It was all about blue skies and radiant sunshine. Durban boasted an average 365 days of pure sunshine. It was endless subtropical summer days, with temperatures above thirty-six degrees Celsius. With such exciting company, the walk was fantastic. The Indian, Coloured, and White suburbs were significantly higher above sea level. We walked down the sprawling Coloured suburb. As we neared the convenience store, we noticed a group of Coloured teenage boys hanging out, sitting on a low wall and socializing. When they spotted us, they whistled. The wolf whistles echoed through the neighbourhood with a loud and penetrating tone. It was obvious that we'd drawn their attention and they found us sexually attractive. I giggled and Ally waved. She spotted a few boys that she knew. Lilly returned the wolf whistles with confidence.

"Are they following us?" asked Iris.

"Yeah, oh yeah!" exclaimed Lilly.

Two of them sung the theme song from *Grease* as they followed us.

> *Summer lovin', had me a blast*
> *Summer lovin', happened so fast*
> *I met a girl crazy for me*

"Stop! And back off!" yelled Ally.

She looked as if she were a sergeant major commanding a battalion or a regiment for matters pertaining to discipline.

Coloured boys were so different from Indian boys. They exuded confidence. Most of them were so handsome in different ways. They carried themselves differently. They had charm, charisma, and natural attractiveness. Most of all they had the swagger. They were more relaxed and at ease with girls. In conversation they were more alert and in tune. They knew how to make the perfect impression and took pride in chatting up girls. Their faces beamed with smiles. They took care of their physical build and wore the right clothing. They were manly, rugged, and handsome.

"That was a terrible, tough call," laughed Iris.

"Those boys are cute, such cutie pies!" cried Lilly.

"Let's not forget we are heading to the park," I laughed.

We giggled and went along, hopping, skipping, and jumping. We crossed over a busy street at the end of the Coloured residential area. Two White men in their early twenties poked their heads out of the pharmacy door, acknowledging our presence. Attraction had no racial barriers.

"They're upcoming pedophiles," giggled Ally.

"Feminine-looking men, as if they're on birth control pills," laughed Iris.

"Good facial structure, good skin, high cheekbones, white teeth, white faces, mmm. Strong jawlines, long, straight noses, mmm," giggled Lilly.

They greeted us with smiles as we entered the White residential area. There were luxurious houses in a prestigious area of the neighbourhood. Those mansions were situated on mountainous terrain. Beautiful huge trees with bright lilac flowers lined the hilly roads. Most notable was that each house had a pond or pool in the front yard that glistened in the radiant sun. The neighbourhood was in close proximity to the beach. Slowly, we climbed up the hilly pavement. The area was so still and so quiet. It was as if we could observe the sounds of silence. We engaged in amazing conversation as we walked along.

We entered the most beautiful park with rocks, water, soil, flora, and fauna. It was fit for royalty or aristocracy. The landscape proclaimed wealth and status, yet it still preserved every sense of nature and was so relaxing. The shade-providing trees, ornamental grounds, and structured lakes were beautiful. The sweeping lawns looked like a green carpet. Several waterfalls added to the splendor. However, the beauty of the park was haunted by the segregation system. The park was divided into White and non-White areas. Even benches in different locations had bold signs. The restaurants at the park were not allowed to serve non-Whites; they were for Whites only. We were thirsty, but we could not drink from a water fountain as it was for Whites only. The public toilets were also segregated, with those at the far end of the park for non-Whites.

We stood at the White area of the park to hear the delightful sounds of children playing on the monkey bars and the swings. They were all White children between the ages of four to six from the neighbourhood. Under a tree there was a group of Black maids who were the most intimate part of a White household. In South Africa the social system was engineered so that each household, in both middle and upper classes, had a Black maid. These maids always dressed in uniforms. They often wore a dress in a pale shade with buttons running down the front, a French maid's apron, and a matching scarf tied around the head. These Black maids became the surrogate parents to children from White families. They united with other maids from different households to socialize at the park, neglecting their duties to watch the children playing. They spoke loudly in their Zulu language, their voices echoing through the park.

"My feet are aching," said Iris.

"Mine too," complained Ally.

"It is those monstrous wedge heels!" cried Lilly.

They plopped themselves on a green bench that had a white sign with black writing that read WHITES ONLY. They sat there smiling as if the bench was God's gift to humanity. I could not take such a bold act and endure any form of racial discipline. I just stood by, warning them of the consequences. The sign proclaimed that the bench was for the use of the White community only. A group of White children headed towards them like a herd of buffalo heading south.

Those "White Only" signs, restricted non-whites from sitting on the park benches.

"You are not allowed to sit on that bench!" they yelled in chorus.

"Do you not see the sign? It is for Whites only!" yelled a five-year-old who I am sure could barely read.

"Get off now!" yelled what looked like a four-year-old.

"Get off! Get off!" they yelled together.

During that dark time, I felt as if it was a liability being an Indian. The White children were aware of their status and security. This was a true tragedy of the cruelty and intolerance of the apartheid regime. Three tall, Coloured teenage girls were being thrown off a park bench by a group of kindergarten children. It felt as if it was forced exile, ironically implemented by little children. The situation was so humiliating. The children were not taught to think about the feelings of another race group. They had such apathy in their voices. They lashed out at us as if we were children ourselves. We had to suffer as victims of abuse at the hands of children because we were the wrong race, the untolerated colour. These children were impulsive, socially dominant, confrontational, and aggressive.

"Get off now, you are not White," squeaked a pint-sized mean girl. "I will call the police." She picked up a little plastic toy phone and role-played a conversation with the police. It was psychologically devastating for us because we were the victims of torture. I saw Ally's face turn red. I knew that anger was building up inside her, triggered by these kindergarten children. Anger limited her ability to follow rules. She was not going to turn away from such wrath. Her dredged feelings from the past surfaced. With a booming voice, she summoned those white kindergarten children to sit in a group on the grass. The Black nannies were so engaged in their conversation that they did not even notice. The brave attitude of the children changed to fear. They were afraid in this unexpected circumstance. Ally rocked their fragile sense of safety.

"Sit down and do not move!" yelled Ally with power in her voice.

The fearful children felt helpless and powerless. They lost the sparkle in their bright blue eyes. They were seized with intense fear.

"Now repeat after me: Bruin hoes are main hoes, and wit hoes are skrik hoes!"

The children repeated after her in a chorus. *Bruin hoes* was South African slang referring to Coloured people. *Wit hoes* referred to white people. *Skrik* was an Afrikaans term meaning frightened. In other words, she wanted them to chant that Coloured people are important people and White people are frightened people. This was Ally's way of getting back at these children and teaching them a lesson. Lilly, Iris, and I giggled as we walked away towards the non-White section of the park. As we left the chant grew louder.

"Bruin hoes are main hoes, and wit hoes are skrik hoes!" the children sang.

We spent an hour relaxing in the non-White area of the park. The company was great and conversation flowed openly. These Coloured girlfriends taught me to be brave, strong, and a fighter. They taught me that I could stand up for myself without an entourage. They taught me the meaning of personal empowerment and accomplishment and to overcome fear. I learned from their friendship about positive thinking and irrational responses to fear. Fear imposes limits on our thinking process and removes our ability to think positively. They taught me about the potentials in life when the crippling emotion of fear is removed. I learned this by watching their experiences in the face of fear. No theoretical knowledge could prepare me to meet fear with such confidence. This was when I dissolved my introvert personality and learned to use that hidden voice to share my opinion. It was a lesson that I took with me into my future.

When we left the park, we passed the White area. As soon as the children saw Ally, they left the swings and monkey bars and ran to the green lawn. They sat down and began chanting: "Bruin hoes are main hoes, and wit hoes are skrik hoes!"

We clapped and cheered them on as we left the park. The walk home was all downhill. We took off our high-wedged sandals and walked on the pavement. We hopped, skipped, danced, and sang as we made our way past the White area. We were teenagers having clean fun. We were like high-spirited horses, so vivacious and lively. Life was full of animation, vigor, and liveliness. Despite the wrath of the apartheid system, we lived life to the fullest, enjoying every moment of the social process of being a teenager. Nothing or nobody could dampen our spirit.

Walking through the luxurious White neighbourhood was a pleasure. We generated high hopes that one day South Africa would be a free nation with racial equalities.

"I'm going to live in that mansion someday," boasted Iris.

"I will be your friendly neighbour in that California-style mansion," gloated Lilly.

Ally complained that she was hot. The coconut palm trees swayed with a gentle breeze. The colour of the late afternoon sun intensified. The summer landscape of each house was appealing. The city of Durban had the reputation of being the hottest place on earth, with temperatures soaring up to 130 degrees Fahrenheit. The bright, blue sky hung over us all day. It was heaven on earth. The ponds and fountains of several homes were a breathtaking vision. The sun stood gloriously in the middle of the sky. Its spiking golden rays, like laser beams, reached the ponds and the crystal surface of the water glistened like precious diamonds. Huge weeping willow trees bent low over the cool ponds. Even the sound of frogs croaking was appealing.

"I am going to dip my hot feet into that pond!" exclaimed Ally.

"Oh no, you're not," I giggled.

Ally was a daredevil, with ultimate courage. She walked up to the pond and stuck her feet right into it. There was nobody around. We giggled like kindergarten children. The situation at that time seemed so hilarious. Ally splashed in the water, trespassing on someone's private property, which was an inch away from the sidewalk. She loved the adrenaline rush. Ally was an impulsive risk taker. Nothing could slow her down.

"You are soaking your Coloured feet in White water!" yelled Iris.

"Just adding a touch of Colour to their pond," said Ally with a roar of laughter.

Suddenly, the lace curtains of the huge bay windows moved. A White man stood there wearing just a pair of boxer shorts. His top half was bare-naked. Anger showed in his bright red face.

"What are you doing?" he yelled in an obnoxiously fierce tone.

A moment of silence filled the air. His right hand moved gently from behind his back. He lifted it up and pointed at Ally, revealing a small black pistol. We ran as fast as our legs could carry us. The gun sent a message that there was no time for apologies. We ran fast and efficiently downhill. Our legs moved with momentum, and gravity did the work. We were so afraid that he was going to fire a shot that we did not even stop or look back. It was really difficult to stop while running down such a steep hill, which just got steeper and steeper. I could feel it in my quad muscles. The fear of speeding downhill was worse than the fear of a gun being pointed at us. We just let gravity do the work. Our concentration was critical because it was difficult to stop when running downhill so fast. I skillfully kept my dynamic motion until I saw a tree. The super-steep hill did not allow me to stop. So I ran towards the tree to stop. The impact was like bouncing off the tree. Iris and Ally copied me. However, Lilly lost her balance and rolled like a rubber tire heading downhill. It was a serious situation. Nevertheless, it left us rolling with laughter.

To us the situation was not tense but hilarious. It was all part of being mischievous teenagers, looking for adventure. We sat at the tree recalling the events: Ally splashing in the pond and the White man's gun. Talking about it seemed more exciting to us than the real experience.

"Drama always brings excitement," said Ally.

"You are the major drama queen," laughed Iris.

We were so happy with an inward feeling of intense joy. We were tickled seeing Lilly rolling with cramps. Our laughter was so contagious that some Black maids passing by stopped and laughed with us, without even knowing what had happened or what we were laughing about. Just our laughter provoked laughter in them. Laughter was like a social interaction that brought Black, Indian, Coloureds, and Whites together in that particular moment. It was our universal human vocabulary because other White folks who passed by began to laugh too, just at the way we were laughing.

CHAPTER 6

A Different Form of Prejudice

Amongst the Indian community, a different form of religious and social class prejudice emerged. The Indian community was divided into different religious groups: Hindus, Muslims, and Christians. The Hindus were further divided into the Tamils, Telegus, Hindustanis, and Gujaratis. All the Hindus attended temples and prayed to the same deities. However, they had different cultural and traditional practices. In addition, they spoke different languages. There were further complications. Each Hindu group had its own caste system, breaking them down into the upper caste, middle caste, and lower caste. The apartheid system in South Africa was complicated, yet not as complicated as the caste segregation. Each caste was not allowed to intermarry. A person born into a particular caste adopted an unchangeable position in society. The castes were ranked according to spiritual purity, lifestyle, and occupation. If upper-caste people married into a lower caste, they were considered to have polluted themselves. Each caste was placed on a social hierarchy based on occupations. Fishermen and domestic workers formed the lower class. Farmers were ranked as the middle class. Priests were the upper class. Above them were kings or royalty. Our generation formed the third- or fourth-generation South Africans. Our great-great-grandparents immigrated to South Africa from India. We were not as familiar with the caste system as our parents or grandparents were. Most of us were "white-washed," with a very European upbringing in South Africa. As the generations passed by, the Indian languages faded away. Everyone communicated through the medium of English, with a strong British accent.

At the all-Indian university, we interacted with each other with no reference to caste. Hindus, Muslims, and Christians were not allowed to intermarry, despite the fact that we were all Indians. Students did not feel the caste inequalities, although their parents or grandparents did. A wide range of intercaste and interreligious relationships emerged at the university. The true test of adherence to ritual purity and caste-based factions surfaced when dealing with marriage.

As a large group, we interacted with each other on a daily basis at the university. Some were couples who stuck together like Siamese twins, while others were single. Nevertheless, we all socialized in one big group. Nelly was a Tamil from an upper caste and she dated Jay who was Hindustani. Their relationship was taboo. They dated openly on campus without their parents knowing. They hung out on campus like a married couple.

"Look at my diamond ring!" boasted Nelly.

"Oh my God, who gave it to you?" asked Rona naively.

"Jay and I are celebrating our first anniversary. We have been dating for one year," she gloated.

"Yes, one year," repeated Jay proudly, blushing at the same time.

"Oh, I am so jealous. When are you going to get me one?" sighed Shireen as she pointed to her boyfriend, Kash.

Shireen and Kash were also in a forbidden relationship. Shireen was Muslim and Kash was Gujarati. They were secretly dating, without their parents' consent. The irony in the situation was Shireen's mother was from the Coloured race. She'd married Shireen's father, who was an Indian Muslim, and converted to Islam. Shireen's mother was a mistress, because Shireen's father had a first wife who was Indian Muslim and he was legally married to her. Shireen and Kash were deeply in love, and they often shared their affections openly in public. They were both wonderful people who deserved each other.

Nelly sat on Jay's lap admiring her beautiful diamond ring, which sparkled. They hugged each other with love and tenderness, and their deep emotional desires were evident. Their love projected such intimacy, compassion, appreciation, and affection. Their passion was obvious, although their relationship was taboo. The university campus was a venue that provided them freedom and self-realization. It was a place where intimacy and romance coexisted. It was a miracle that they were able to keep their relationship from their parents and other relatives.

"To celebrate I am going to treat all of you to lunch!" said Jay excitedly.

"Lets have our favourite Indian-style french fries," laughed Rona.

"I'll buy the soft drinks," said Kash.

We huddled together in a group. There were several plates of french fries in front of us. We called them "chips." We garnished them with vinegar, salt, and a pungent chili powder. A few of us ordered grilled cheese sandwiches with sweet corn. This was our favourite meal for lunch each day. Just seeing it stimulated my taste buds.

Jay and Nelly hailed from the same caste. However, they were prohibited from marrying under the guidelines of religious conflict. Nelly was Tamil and Jay was Hindustani. Nelly feared that she could be badly beaten by her parents if they found out about Jay. The couple's only alternative for marriage was to elope. This conservative social dictum existed between all Indians. Even relatives who formed the extended family unit expected young people to follow the strict social code and dictated to them about their future marital partners. Jay's family was no different. They expected him to marry a traditional Hindustani girl. Nevertheless, months had passed by and Jay and Nelly had continued to be the perfect couple. They'd managed to hide the dark secret from their families. This was not a rare phenomenon amongst mixed couples in the Indian community. Nelly and Jay were both intellectuals and career oriented, but it did not matter. They felt the intense need to be close.

For a few days, Nelly and Jay were absent from university, which was odd because their attendance had always been excellent.

"Did you talk to Nelly?" I asked Rona.

"No. It's so strange. I called her home several times and her mom just hung up on me," said Rona.

"How about Jay, have any of you spoken with him?" asked Shireen.

"No," we all chorused.

We were worried about Nelly and Jay, but we had no control over the situation. We all had a sixth sense that they were in trouble. Several rumors surfaced that Nelly's parents had found out about their relationship and she was under house arrest. We learned that her parents refused to let her out of the house unless she terminated her relationship with Jay. Trouble brewed like a witch's stew. The air felt contaminated.

Jay returned to university after a week. He stayed away from our group. He spent most of his time sitting alone at the pond. Jay was heartbroken and going through a period of mourning. It was a great period of adjustment for him because he was not just losing Nelly, he could not sit with friends either. Seeing his former flame would bring back emotions, which he tried to avoid at all cost.

"I saw Jay at the pond," said Shireen.

"Did you talk with him?" I asked.

"Yes, I did, but he cried so much. His eyes were as red as the sunset. He's lost a lot of weight. It seems as if he's lost more hair as well. He is balding at the top, like a bald eagle," said Shireen.

Jay's broken heart cut him like a knife. No matter how we tried to console him when we saw him, it did not help. There was no way that he could reconcile with Nelly because they were in a forbidden relationship. Since there was no chance of making up, he had to suffer a broken heart. He looked for solutions to heal his broken heart. He could not turn his feelings off like a switch. The more advice we gave him, the worse he seemed to feel. It was an irreversible breakup, which was enough to indicate that their relationship had been taboo. He had lost his soul mate.

Nelly took a semester off and returned during the next semester. She had lost a lot of weight. What surprised us the most was that she'd cut her long, curly hair. Most Indian parents did not allow their daughters to cut their hair. I believed that Nelly wanted a change after such an emotional breakup. It was as if she'd cut her nose to spite her face. She'd had enough time at home to grieve.

"Is everything OK?" asked Shireen.

"My parents are watching me closely. A cousin saw Jay and I at the movies and she told her parents, who immediately called mine. Then hell broke loose," cried Nelly.

"What drama! Sounds like a soap opera," I commented.

"It must have been love—but it's over now!" sang Nelly.

"My parents are going to arrange a marriage for me. They are looking around for a suitor…husband," stuttered Nelly.

"I am sure that when they exploded, you must have imploded!" I commented wittily.

"Yes, the walls caved in!" Nelly sobbed and laughed at the same time.

It was odd to see Jay pass by without even stopping to say hello. The breakup was too painful for him. Nelly managed to minimize her anguish while mourning the loss of her relationship. She was prepared to move on to a new phase of her life, without Jay. We were the perfect support network for her. However, Jay seemed to be all alone, shattered by the breakup. His sorrow was evident, as he walked by in an almost fetal position. Jay and Nelly developed that emotional distance, although the environment could not change. Their dark days were evident. The journey that they'd traveled together had come to an abrupt end, and they felt the loss. Nelly began to explore her identity outside of the relationship, and we provided her with emotional support. She displayed a multitude of emotions—anger, denial, joy, shock, depression, anxiety, and relief. We had to deal with her mood fluctuations.

I felt like a counselor helping Nelly deal with her destructive impulses and offering her the comfort she needed. At intervals she listened attentively but did the opposite of what I advised her. That frustrated me. We needed to return to our routine as soon as possible. I encouraged her to think about Jay's negative traits to help her heal faster. That semester I had a conflict with my courses. I could not take psychology during the day because it clashed with my communication course. That meant longer days on campus. I had to stay on campus to take my psychology course at night. Nelly had the same problem. I was happy to have her company while all of our friends left early.

The psychology course at night was different from our morning classes, which were filled with teenagers and young adults. I was surprised to see so many older people in the night lectures. A lot of them were teachers upgrading courses. There were students in their forties, fifties, and even sixties. Most of them had attended teacher's college. They were studying for their new degrees. The dynamics of the lecture were different, with more open discussions. Nelly and I felt so immature. However, we developed many friendships as we became familiar with those around us. Age had no boundaries. We studied as one intimate group.

Most notable was a tall student called Sunny. He was about five years older than we were. He was a gym teacher at a high school. We all sat at the same tables in the lecture auditorium. He became our instant friend as we shared lecture notes and studied together. He also hung out with Nelly and me when we ate dinner at the cafeteria. We spent time researching at the library and chatting at the pond. He had a teaching diploma from teacher's college and was there to get his degree. Each day after school, he would meet us at the university cafeteria.

As weeks passed by, I noticed that Nelly had become closer to him. When they met each day, they gazed at each other in a romantic and flirtatious manner. It made me uncomfortable when they engaged in their playful overture. Their display indicated that there was a deeper relationship between them. Sunny used qualities of gallantry and chivalry to charm Nelly. I sensed a mild form of intimacy between them. Nelly's body language had changed from depression to the flicking of her hair, subtle touching, romantic eye contact, and romantic nudging. Even her voice, its intonation and volume, had changed. I could not believe what my eyes perceived because she was on the rebound. As the days progressed, the flirting indicated a deeper romantic relationship. At first it was just amusement, but it soon reached a stage where their glances said a million words. Sunny took the initiative and Nelly just went along. I thought that she would repulse such advances by Sunny, however I noticed a different type of courtship. This was far from my etiquette rules, and I felt like a fifth wheel on a four-wheeled car. I tried to concentrate on the lecturer. It was difficult because I was right next to them.

Nelly had entered troubled waters once more. Sunny was Gujarati and she was Tamil, which meant that their relationship was taboo. In addition, her parents did not tolerate romantic love. Her parents stuck firmly to the patriarchy and caste-based rules of Hinduism. They were strong believers in maintaining family alliances through arranged marriages. The gradual demise of arranged marriages existed amongst the younger generation of South African Indians. There was an inexorable rise of love marriages. However, Nelly's family was set on finding her a prospective partner.

"I think I am falling in love!" confessed Nelly one day.

"How about your relationship with Jay?" I asked.

"Oh, that is history," she replied.

"Your heart is on the rebound, and you do not know much about Sunny. Furthermore, he is Gujarati," I said, trying to knock some sense into her.

"Oh, well!" she exclaimed.

"You know, Nelly, you are the typical 'ask-hole.' You ask for advice and you do exactly the opposite of what I tell you!" I retorted.

"Are you calling me an a—hole?" she asked with disgust.

"No, *ask-hole*! When I advise you, you push a towel through one ear, pull it out the other ear, and move it left to right, erasing all the advice. That frustrates me! You get the satire and irony?" I giggled.

"But I do not want to be alone!" she replied in a child-like tone.

"You rather be alone, than be with someone and wish you were alone. Now by that I mean you can be miserable with someone and wish you were not with them!" I advised her.

"You are so sarcastic!" she slurred.

"That's because, metaphorically, you are a loose cannon!" I replied in an ironic tone.

"A loose cannon?" she asked with a confused look.

"You run around looking for love in all the wrong places. Looking for love in too many places!" I felt like a maternal figure, advising a child about the law of romantic nature.

Psychologically, Nelly was incapable of making reasonable decisions regarding a suitable boyfriend. She displayed emotional neediness. I knew that her lingering feelings towards Jay were not over. It was her desire to deal with her emotional instability. It seemed like an intense desire to distract herself from her painful breakup. Her tumultuous emotions were still visible. She found refuge in Sunny. Her heart was still battered and bruised, yet she claimed to be in love. It was only in hindsight that I acknowledged what she had denied.

I perceived Sunny as a player. His charm and charisma were visible. My instinct told me that he was a womanizer. He'd managed to seduce Nelly, and she was captured in his web of love.

71

I was afraid to warn her because she thought that I was jealous or envious of her newfound love. But an inner intuitive instinct told me that Sunny was a player. He was good-looking and confident. He was lighter in skin complexion, which attracted most Indian girls. We had the choice of fifty shades of brown in our selection of men. He had the swag in his walk and he knew when to play the trump card. He was alert and attentive when a woman spoke. His conversation was smooth, and he had the right words in the right places. He displayed wit and humour. He always dotted his Is and crossed his Ts with his perfect verbal communication skills. By that I mean he tried to articulate using perfect grammar. To me he was too good to be true, and I smelled a rat. He was a fictional character in a real world. I knew that he had the guile and charm to seduce women. When Nelly spoke he was amorously and gallantly attentive.

"He gives me so much attention, affection, and appreciation," slurred the love-sick Nelly.

"Just be careful. However, I am happy for you," I consoled her. In my mind I thought that some village had lost its idiot. "To trust or not to trust?" I recited my soliloquy.

"To be or not to be? To live or to die?" giggled Nelly.

"Yes, you dig your own grave and sometimes bury yourself!" I exclaimed with irony in my tone.

Just then Sunny walked in with his swag. He smelled fresh, doused in Calvin Klein's Eternity perfume. Each day he seemed to dress younger and more fashionably. He wore a dark pair of blue jeans, a white V-neck T-shirt and a short black leather jacket with the collar turned up. He looked around, greeted others around him, and then headed straight for Nelly. He had this significant cluster of body movements, showing her that he was interested in her. He stared at her with many preening, romantic gestures. He stroked his chin and pursed his lips. He tilted his entire torso and listened intently to Nelly. I looked away with disgust. I felt as if I were watching some Indian movie where the romantic notions were present. He gazed at her lips as if he wanted a kiss. He strummed her face with his fingers, his eyes dilating. His dark pupils got even bigger. He intimately stroked the palm of her right hand. His body language gave her the cues that he was romantically interested in her. All I could imagine was some soppy Indian song playing and seeing them dancing around some brightly coloured, flowery trees, which symbolized love-making in Indian movies. Then from the top of the hills or green pasture, a little boy would run in slow motion and Nelly and Sunny would caress him with such tenderness. The birth of their baby, as played in an Indian movie. I giggled at the thought and imagined them in slow motion.

"What's so funny?" asked Nelly.

"Oh, just what the lecturer said," I laughed.

"What was that?" she naively asked.

"Concentrate!" I exclaimed.

Nelly continued to orchestrate the pace and flow of her romantic relationship. Sunny continued to be the master of emotional manipulation and lured Nelly into a physical relationship. I was able to gauge the emotional temperature of the lecture auditorium quicker than a flash of lightning. I was good at deciphering body language, with obvious signals. I knew that Sunny and Nelly were much more than just friends. I concentrated on the lecturer and learned to ignore their romantic moves in the lecture room. I wondered if Sunny had yet delivered Nelly his autobiography.

CHAPTER 7

Infidelity

Months passed by and my friends, Sher and Tonyia, invited me to a house party. They were my party buddies, and we often went to clubs and house parties together. The three of us did not have boyfriends, so we enjoyed the single scene. We enjoyed the loud music, dancing, and consumption of alcohol. I found house parties more intimate and cozy than going to nightclubs. Often parents were present; however, in most cases they were in the kitchen preparing the snacks or meal and chatting with other adults. The fun, food, and friends dazzled me.

The DJ broke out the latest music, and we all danced on a huge dance floor at the back of Sher's house. The spotlight was on us as we danced to the beat. We were like live electric wires. The music was our guide, and we moved our bodies along with the rhythm. The music took us away, to paradise. We had fun snapping our fingers and swaying our bodies.

Tonyia, who was short, chubby, and tomboy-like, enjoyed clapping to draw attention to herself. She was Muslim and Sher was Hindustani. We always teased Tonyia for drinking because Muslim girls did not drink. We moved with the traditional steps and gestures of "YMCA" by the Village People. The Bee Gees kept us alive and rocking to their music. We moved in groups doing the steps of the macarena, which allowed us to go crazy and wild. It was all part of the fun. Tonyia imitated Michael Jackson as his song "Thriller" played. We all felt close and comfortable on the dance floor as everyone joined in. Everyone got loose and accustomed to the moves. Sher's aunts and uncles joined in, doing the salsa and the swing. We randomly chitchatted while dancing, making the evening even more exciting. We sang along to our favourite songs. Alcohol allowed some to loosen up on the dance floor. Sher, Tonyia, and I were accustomed to letting ourselves open up, and we always had ultimate fun together.

"Stop the music, dinner's ready!" yelled Sher's mother.

"Come on, Tonyia and Kay, let's stuff ourselves," yelled Sher as she led us to the backyard, where dinner was being served.

"Yippee—food, my favourite subject!" exclaimed Tonyia as she sprinted towards the buffet table.

There was a variety of food. I amused myself with the selection of Indian cuisine. With all the unique, spicy Indian delights, I did not exercise moderation. I was under the spell of South Asian masalas and curries. It was like practising an Indian ritual with channa masala, biryani, tandoori chicken, chicken curry, fluffy white basmati rice, samosas, vadas, roti, curried potato, and a variety of Indian desserts. The sight of the food alleviated the line-up boredom, as I had fantasies of sampling every dish in sight. The exotic smell of spices and herbs filled the air and activated my taste buds. A segment of the buffet offered the most exotic vegetarian dishes. I could smell the exquisite aromas of garam masala, cumin, jeera, turmeric, ginger, coriander, garlic, mint, curry leaves, cardamom, saffron, nutmeg, and fenugreek (methi) rising from the heavily spiced foods. South African Indians enjoyed their different indigenous styles of food, with regional variations. It was part of our heritage and hospitality. Food was an integral part of our celebrations, and the Indian community prepared it elaborately. It was part of our ethic identity that we prepared food with such pride. Sher's mother had cooked a unique blend of Tamil, Hindustani, Gujarati, and Muslim Indian food, which made it difficult to choose.

As I reached out for the dorsa served with chutney and sambar, a typical Tamil dish, I heard a familiar voice. On the opposite side of the table was Sunny. He had a nervous expression on his face.

"Hey, Sunny, how are you?" I yelled out excitedly.

"Fine," he replied, avoiding eye contact.

"Where is Nelly?" I asked in the same excited tone as he ignored my question.

"Who is that?" asked the girl next to him demonically.

"An acquaintance from my psychology class," he replied in a nervous tone.

He ignored me, and I sensed that he was extremely uncomfortable. He choked on his food as the girl next to him rubbed his back vigorously and intimately. She was a chubby, unattractive Indian girl as tall as he was. She attacked him with a series of questions about me, as if she needed concrete evidence for peace of mind. Sunny was in a competitive situation, and I felt as if I had infringed upon his territory. His code of conduct was so different. At university he was very friendly, with a loud bombastic voice. At the party he looked like a tortoise withdrawing into its shell. I wondered if he was bipolar schizophrenic.

With a plate stacked with food, I walked towards Sher and Tonyia, who were seated away from the table. The DJ played soft and romantic music. The huge, silver, mirrored disco ball shed rays of coloured light on each person's face. The night was dark. Beautiful green stars that shone like emeralds filled the sky. It was a hot summer's night. I plopped myself next to Sher.

"Something strange! Do you know that tall chap standing close to the buffet table?" I asked Sher since it was her house party.

"Yes, that's my distant relative, Sunny. Why do you ask?" She seemed confused.

"He is in my psychology class, and he is dating my friend Nelly. You have not met her," I whispered.

"That's not possible. The chubby, tall girl standing next to him is his wife, Betty. He married a Christian girl two years ago," said Sher.

"Oh my God, what a cheater!" I exclaimed.

"Infidelity? Adultery?" stuttered Sher.

Tonyia, who was listening to our conversation, yelled out in a drunken voice as she looked at Sunny, "Who is Nelly? Cheater!"

Sunny looked at me nervously. He knew that the cat was out of the bag. Tonyia, Sher, and I stared at him with disgust.

"Beguiler, deceiver, slicker, trickster, bluffer, [*bleep, bleep, bleep, bleep*]!" I angrily uttered every profanity under the moonlit sky.

It was not just an unprovoked accusation or anonymous information. He'd publicly vented his feelings for Nelly. Falling in love on the rebound hindered her ability to deal with a relationship so soon. I could not even perceive the ramifications of such news for Nelly. Telling her was a short-term solution; the complex issues of coping with it would have to be her long-term problem. I was the only vehicle to expose Sunny, and I felt the burden. He'd violated all the rules of marriage. I could not believe that Sunny had engaged in an extramarital affair. After dinner Sher, Tonyia and I decided to leave the party. I was not comfortable being in the same room as Sunny. We asked Sher's parents for permission, and we headed for the Durban beach. After a night of clubbing or partying, most people hung out at the beach, where we met more of our friends and acquaintances from university.

When I broke the news to Nelly, she had a strange attitude.

"I found out that Sunny is married," I informed her.

"I just came out of one relationship, and I know that I've found my prince," she continued.

"You know, Albert Einstein once said that you cannot solve problems with the same thinking that caused the problems," I said.

"What do you mean?" she asked with the same naïve tone.

"Stop playing the victim! You are the cause of your own problems. Now, change the way you think and solve this problem. The solution is in the palm of your hand," I advised her.

"You sound like some old philosopher," she smirked.

"You need to have an inner dialogue with yourself. Talk to yourself and come up with the solution to your problem," I continued, as if talking to a brick wall.

She did not want to believe me. I figured that Sunny had lied to her. She did not believe that he was married. I wondered if she did not care that she was dating a married man as long as his wife did not know. I believed in the law of karma and wondered about it coming around. Weeks passed by and I noticed that they still hung out together. I avoided them and spent more time at the library. During lectures I sat at the back of the auditorium to avoid them.

However, in less than a week I heard that Nelly's parents had arranged a marriage for her. This time she had to curtail the process of courtship. I perceived that it was a forced marriage. The nature and duration of the time from their meeting to the engagement was about one month. Nelly's parents saw Calvin as their daughter's potential spouse. The parents retained the prerogative to arrange a quick marriage. I did not know if they had found out about Nelly's relationship with Sunny. I could not imagine why they would rush her into marriage. Calvin was of the same caste and religious group as Nelly, so the parents were happy with the match. They were traditional Tamil parents, so dating was not prevalent. Nelly had to conform due to the pressure from her parents. I did not know Calvin personally, but I had seen him at several clubs and parties. I knew that he was related to my friend Rona. I could not imagine him in an arranged marriage because he was so modern in his approach to life. He was good-looking and tall. I knew that he dated a lot of girls. He was a player. However, Indian boys in most cases listened and went along with their mother's choice. Conversely, Nelly was more conservative in her physical features and in the way she dressed. It seemed that the intergenerational relationship between the two families was more important than the marital relationship. Nelly's parents were only interested in the stability and endurance of the family. The hereditary caste system also played an important role in their arranged marriage. They did not believe in intercaste marriages.

We thought that the apartheid system was difficult to cope with. However, the period of arranged marriages was another era of error. The caste system also reduced social equality. The focus was solely on caste stratification. In the urban culture of South Africa, modern arranged marriages were based on pragmatic considerations. They did not involve traditional male-female duties. Parents felt the arranged marriage was the only way to choose a right partner for their son or daughter in order to avoid future divorce. Calvin and Nelly belonged to the upper caste of Brahmins, who belonged to the radical Vedic group of people. A Brahmin belonged to the group of priests, seers, and philosophers. In traditional India they gained positions of power and belonged to a wealthy group. They followed various branches of the Vedas in the Hindu society. In addition, the Vedas exemplified the truth of external validity. Caste systems were also observed among the followers of other religious groups in different generations in South Africa. Ironically, the segregation seen amongst the various religious Indian groups paralleled the segregation brought about by the apartheid system in South Africa.

Nelly's Indian wedding was an exotic event filled with rituals and celebration, which continued for a week. The traditional Indian wedding brought families together to form a close social network. It was a happy occasion, yet with a solemn overtone. The couple sat onstage in front of a bright exotic fire, following all that the priest ordered. It was a ceremony where they exchanged nuptials and the priest purified their minds, bodies, and souls.

Nelly wore the most beautiful sari, in red georgette with contrasting gold sequins, beads, and stonework. The embroidery was exotic and gaudy. The border was embellished with an intricate sequin and bead design that shimmered under the bright lights. Her marvelous sari completed her joyous experience on such a special occasion. Those six meters of exotic fabric draped over her body in elegant style. She looked fabulous. She wore the most intricate gold jewelry, simultaneously satisfying all the traditional demands and her ingrained desire for such extravagant ornamentation.

Calvin wore a beige turban, which had been an integral part of the South African Indian ethos for decades, an ancient tradition we strived to keep alive through the generations. It was the symbol of royal demeanor. It was sensuous and graceful, which suited his masculine profile. He looked splendid, exuding a royal aura.

Nelly stretched out her hands to hold on to the coconut given to her by the priest. Her elegant fingers were adorned with the most exotic henna patterns. The setting was colorful, vibrant, and elaborate. It was a majestic event, with dazzling stage decorations. Delicate fabrics draped the stage, adding to the glamour of such an auspicious occasion. Every tasteful touch added to the magnanimity and distinction of the situation while still maintaining the Indian ethnicity and glamour expected of both the bridal couple and their families. The bridal families ascended the stage with class and style, revealing rare blends of ethnic fashions in their ensembles.

Despite the cheerful spirit of the occasion, I could not help but notice the expression on Nelly's face. She was glum throughout the ceremony. At times tears streamed down her flushed cheeks. At other times she gave an instant giggle when she could not pronounce the Indian words uttered by the priest.

At times she seemed annoyed by the attention given to her by the bridal party. It seemed as if she was getting married without her consent or against her will. The differences between Calvin and Nelly were distinct. She was more of the conservative type while he was an extrovert.

The apartheid system in South Africa was part of the human rights abuse. Ironically, the marriage violated the principles of freedom and autonomy for both Nelly and Calvin. Through the pressure of their families, they were forced to consent to marriage. They were ordered to marry to meet the goals of belonging to the same religious group and caste system. It was a sad extreme. They had to learn how to balance matrimony with love. The intimidation showed on Nelly's face. However, Calvin seemed to play into the role of restoring social honor to his parents. The parental pressure that caused the pair to marry was evident. Family pride and social obligation was what brought the couple together in matrimony. They felt a sense of duty to marry each other. They were coerced into marriage, and there was no room for negotiations. In the Indian community, the entire nuclear and extended family participated in arranging marriages between couples. However, forced marriages had garnered little attention in South Africa during a critical political era. Marriage became a crosscultural and crossracial issue in South Africa, a means of preserving culture.

CHAPTER 8

Pride and Prejudice

There were some Indian families who were more modern in their thinking and allowed their children to date or enter into a love marriage. There were others with a common modus operandi. Their method of operation was to: find a wealthy suitor for their daughters so that the family would maintain a high economic status in life. Marriage was a means of maintaining honor, even if the young girl was in mortal danger. Forced marriages amongst the Indian community was not just a heterosexual issue. Indian parents felt forced marriage was a cure for gay and lesbian couples, a method of curing them of their disease. A cousin of mine fled the country soon after his graduation because he was gay. It was his way of dealing with such turmoil and mental health issues. It was a matter that dampened his parents' pride. He was stuck in the closet and could not escape. He had to deal with his parents' pride and society's prejudice.

I always thought that my friend Tonyia was a lesbian, but I was afraid to ask. On one occasion I received a frantic call from her. She seemed to be in a state of depression and urgently needed to talk to a friend. She came over to my home in split-seconds. We drove to the beachfront, where we could privately talk. She was upset and tears rolled down her cheeks. I wondered if she was ready to come out of the closet.

"What's the matter?" I asked with tenderness in my voice.

"It is a secret that I have been harbouring for almost a year," she cried.

"Are you a lesbian?" I asked seriously.

"No. Oh no. How stupid of you to think so," she giggled.

"Well, you are such a tomboy. And so butch," I added.

"It's Calvin," she whispered, as if the car had ears.

"Calvin—Nelly's husband?" I exclaimed with confusion.

"Yes, *the* Calvin," she said with a sarcastic tone.

I hung out with Tonyia at house parties and clubs. She was not at university. Sher, Tonyia, and I had a fantastic friendship. My best friend, Cherry, did not know them. It was a different clique that I hung out with off campus. Tonyia went on to explain that she and Calvin had formed a platonic friendship years ago. They were magical friends who confided in each other and helped solve each other's problems. Feelings of love had emerged, and her relationship with Calvin had evolved into a sexual relationship. To Calvin it was more on unemotional terms, whereas Tonyia was fully emotionally involved in the relationship. With such genuine platonic love, they inspired each other's minds and souls. Just Calvin's physical form and the timbre of his voice triggered goose bumps in Tonyia.

"When was the last time you saw him?" I asked.

"Just last night," she cried.

"Was it physical?" I continued.

"Yes, it involved sex!" she exclaimed.

"Tonyia, are you crazy? He is married to Nelly. I understand that you knew him long before she did, but he is a married man!" I yelled with such shock.

"I know," was all she had to say.

"And the plot thickens!" I exclaimed.

"How can something so wrong seem so right?" she cried.

"You need to take an inventory of your life. Keep the good and eliminate the bad," I advised her.

Once again I felt uncomfortable. I enjoyed playing the role of psychiatrist, however it did lead me to difficult situations. I felt the guilt of holding Tonyia's burden. At the same time, Nelly and I were friends on campus. Our friendship had grown around going to lectures together and hanging out during our spare time. We did not socialize off campus. Nevertheless, now I had to keep a secret from her that involved her husband. When I'd found out that Sunny was married, it had been easy to tell her because they were just dating. Furthermore, she did not believe me at first and continued with the relationship. But I could not tell her about Calvin and Tonyia because I did not want to be the cause of her marriage falling apart. I did not want to infringe upon her personal space.

"This has to be karma," I said.

"You mean Nelly had an affair with a married man, Sunny? And now it's her husband doing the same?" asked Tonyia.

"Exactly, you took the words right out of my mouth," I replied. "Tonyia, you have to end this relationship. Set him free; if he comes back to you then he is yours. If he does not, then he never was!"

I could not spill my guts or be candid. I found myself in a dilemma. I tried to discourage Tonyia by telling her that she deserved a man of her own who would give her love, attention, affection, and appreciation. I did not know Calvin personally, so I had no way of talking to him. It was impossible for Tonyia to marry Calvin because she was Muslim and he was Tamil. So their relationship was taboo anyway. I felt like a judge in a friendship court. I had to weigh in on a friend's worst nightmare. I wished I had a jury to back me up. I risked the fact that Nelly could find out. I could not believe that I was involved in such a cheating dilemma. I found myself in a tough spot, with no escape. It was a secret that I had to hold on to. I wished that Tonyia had not consulted me or confided in me. I was tangled in a series of soap operas. I was a strong believer in karma and knew that someday Calvin would have to pay for such infidelity.

The next day I arrived at university bearing the burden of the secret on my shoulders. I felt like I was walking with a slouch, thinking about what I was told the night before. From the car park to the main campus there were lots of stairs to climb. I did not even feel the climb because I was so deep in thought. The stairs seemed to go on forever. Each stair was like a symbol of a secret that I embraced, holding the intellectual light of my wisdom and truth. As I ascended I felt elevated, as if I were reaching a more cognitive illumination. The stairs were symbolic of my thoughts, and as I reached a higher sphere, I felt spiritual enlightenment, which allowed me to think about solutions to my problems. I stepped onto a wide landing and observed the next flight of stairs that I had to ascend.

At the top of those stairs was Shireen. I observed her as she walked towards the stairs. Her movements were slow. She walked with her head bowed. She looked as if she was down in the dumps. She was usually vibrant, animated, and bubbly. I could not understand what would trigger such behaviour in her. It was unusual to see her alone, without Kash. She had lost a lot of weight, which looked fatal. She was always at the ideal body weight, with a perfect figure carried around in a small frame. It seemed to me as if she was in a potentially harmful situation. She noticed me but did not smile. She was a sad soul as she descended, as if she carried a great burden on her back. Just her walk down those stairs symbolized transformation and change. She seemed to be in a lower level of consciousness, as denoted by her body movement. Her movement was indicative of a negative flow of energy.

"Hi there, where is your other half?" I yelled out.

"We are not together, we broke up." Tears streamed down her bony cheeks.

"Oh my God, I am so sorry. What can I do to cheer you?" I asked.

She just shrugged her shoulders. Kash's mother was responsible for breaking up the relationship. Kash was Gujarati and his mother expected him to marry a Gujarati girl. Shireen was Muslim and Kash's mother disapproved of her. Kash was close to graduating with a degree in engineering. His mother had arranged a marriage for him. The unknown girl was graduating as a doctor, and most of all, she was Gujurati as well. Kash was really close to his mother, therefore he felt obligated to meet his mother's wishes. This news came as a shock to me because Shireen and Kash shared such a close relationship. I hadn't visualized them apart. They had been dating for almost four years. It was sad to hear about the end of their relationship. Shireen's life seemed to be in decay. I hugged her fragile frame to show sympathy and empathy.

"I am here for you, please call me when you are down. We can get together," I consoled her.

"I'll try," she said, "but for now I prefer to be alone. Too many memories," she solemnly spoke.

"You have been skipping lectures?" I asked.

"There are those mornings when I just cannot get out of bed," she cried.

"Time will heal," I replied.

I felt so sorry for Shireen. She had no greater awareness of where she was and the steps she could take to heal. Her self-esteem was low. Her activities were not congruent with my expectations, so it was difficult to offer her advice. It was almost as if she were in a state of spiritual decay, which was terrible. I was susceptible to feeling her pain, and I wished that she could overcome her problem by looking for a more fruitful experience. She had established a close friendship with Kash. She was so tangible in front of me, but I could not measure what was in her heart at that particular moment. Being late for my lecture prompted me to say a hasty good-bye. I promised her that I would call her that night. Marrying across the caste, class, and religious system was just as difficult as coping with the laws of the apartheid system. I wished that I could stay with Shireen, but she'd signaled that she wanted to be alone. Plus, I could not skip my statistics lecture because the lecturer took attendance. I ran along as fast as my legs would carry me.

A week passed and it was difficult reaching Shireen. She did not take calls. She was going through the most painful experience in her life, and there was no miraculous solution that I could offer her. All I could do was try to give her the hope and inspiration to move on. She could not see beyond the horizon and did not allow herself time for personal growth. She could not take a personal inventory because she'd been in a perfect relationship with Kash. She'd met him in her first year of university; therefore, she had never experienced single life on campus. She'd become a young adult whilst in a relationship. Therefore, she had no insights as how to move ahead. It was imperative that she have time to grieve. She had no confident anticipation about her future without Kash. I could not propel her into a period of frantic change. It was a painful breakup. She cried from her poisonous pain because she knew that there was no room for a makeup. Kash's mother was preparing a gigantic wedding. Therefore, Shireen had no happiness to pursue.

Soon I received a call from a friend saying that Shireen was at the hospital. The very next morning I rushed there. I met Rona at the parking lot.

"What happened?" I frantically asked.

"She attempted suicide!" she cried.

"Is she all right?" I asked.

"No, she is brain-dead. No hope, it looks like," she cried.

"Hope, hope, hope," I stuttered.

"Her family members are with her, so do not ask them any questions because they are devastated," she begged.

"I won't," I replied sadly.

Rona went on to explain that early that morning Shireen had gone into the bathroom to prepare for university. That was her morning ritual. She did not come out of the bathroom when her sister knocked on the door. Her sister could not hear any running water, so she forcibly opened the door. Shireen hung from the shower rack with her scarf around her neck. The scarf had stretched and she was almost in a sitting position on the bathtub. The family called the emergency unit and she was rushed to the hospital.

I walked down the long corridor. It was like walking through an ivory tunnel. The corridor seemed so long as my emotions ran high. A nurse led me into Shireen's private room. Her close family members stood up to greet me. Her sister hugged me with such grief and sobbed hysterically. Everyone present in the room sobbed too. Her other sister plucked up the courage to tell me that Shireen was brain-dead. I stood at the right side of Shireen's bed and stroked her chin. Her chest moved up and down as if she was breathing.

"It's the machines keeping her body alive," sobbed her sister. "This morning her kidneys failed."

I fought back the tears, and I was simply speechless. Shireen looked so different on the bed, her face so swollen. She had gauze over both eyes and different plastic tubes through her mouth. I stroked her cheeks, hoping she would twitter or even move, but her lifeless body lay there with no emotions. She was in a persistent vegetative state. The life-support equipment maintained all her bodily functions. She was in an irreversible coma. The equipment kept her body's metabolic system working, which gave her family some hope that she was physically with them. There was no clinical evidence of brain function, though. The doctors felt that it was an inappropriate time to withdraw life support because of the emotional status of her family. This was one moment when I questioned death; I did not know how to define it. My eyes became blurry, and warm tears ran down my cheeks. The voluminous tears rapidly moved me towards sorrow as I felt the stress of losing a good friend who could not face the trials and tribulations of life. That night I had a good cry.

The next day I stood at the door of the funeral parlor. My legs could not move. The strong smell of incense sticks made its way out the door as the priest did his rituals. I was not there to celebrate her life but to mourn her death. Sanctifying Shireen's death was not easy. The most beautiful array of flowers in bright shades of pink, yellow, and red surrounded the casket. Loud wailing was the only sound. Slowly but surely I made my way down the aisle. As I drew nearer to the casket, the wailing grew stronger. I could feel the pain of her parents and sisters as I bent down to console them. I offered them my condolences.

Shireen lay in her white casket. Her eyes were closed. Her long eyelashes were visible, and she looked like Sleeping Beauty. She wore a white satin dress with gold threads. Her arms were crossed over her chest, and she caressed a fluffy, beige teddy bear. She had a smirk on her face, as if to say that she was content with death. I stared at her. At that very moment I felt so angry. I was so angry that she chose to take her life so soon.

My mind was filled with the question, "Why, why, why, why—why?" as if I were expecting her to get up and provide me with the answer. I remembered my last words to her: "I will call you."

I did not get the chance to do so. I was not prepared to say good-bye. I turned around and walked towards a seat in the middle of the room. I spotted several friends, but I did not want to sit close to them. They were crying, and we were like strangers in an unfamiliar setting.

I recalled Shireen's last words to me, that she wanted to be alone. That is exactly the way I felt then; I wanted to be alone. I was there to share my love, respect, and grief. Being alone helped me to face Shireen's death. Her rituals were conducted according to religious denomination. I felt the intolerable pain. Intense emotions filled my heart and I felt a sense of unreality, as if I were enclosed in a cocoon. I felt the tightness in my throat as tears streamed down my face. There was a shortness of breath, and extreme fatigue took over my body. It was an emotional upheaval, which I was not prepared for. I felt that Shireen had not valued the preciousness of life because, to her, death was inevitable.

A cousin of Shireen's went up onstage to deliver her funeral oration: "Dear family and friends, we are gathered here to celebrate the life and mourn the death of Shireen, our dear cousin, friend, and family member…. We will call upon a few close friends to give a speech."

All I heard was my name. I wiped away my tears and plucked up the courage to walk up to the podium.

"My beloved friend defiantly watches me from above, and I have written a poem to say my final farewell:

> To you, dear friend, farewell.
> You did not want to tell
> The sorrow you felt inside.
> Why did you not confide?
> I said my last good-bye
> On that day I saw you cry.
> I held your hand with sympathy,
> My heart was filled with empathy.
> I did not know your life would cease,
> I know that you're in a place of peace.
> I vow to think of you every day,
> In my thoughts and when I pray.
> The pain I feel is so deep,
> Your loss makes me want to weep.
> Absence makes my heart grow fonder.
> Your departure makes me wonder,
> Why did you leave me with such pain?
> And your death drives me insane.
> I hear the tone of your timid voice,

You know that you had a better choice.
Together we could have grown old.
Why did your life turn so bitter cold?
Bringing your life to an abrupt end.
To you my sweet love I send.
I experience the stages of grief,
Death was your only relief.
I remember your passionate smile,
I remember your immaculate style,
Times when you confided in me.
It's so hard to set you free.
I feel your presence standing by,
In my dreams you did not die.
Your protection makes me strong,
Life for me would not go wrong.
My memories of you remain vivid,
Your sudden death made me so livid.
You are able to see good from bad,
Your passing makes me feel so sad.
Seeing your life as a visual slide,
Someday we'll meet on the other side.
For now this pain I will endure,
Such grief has no immediate cure.
I love you with all my heart,
I regret the day we had to part.
Your presence in spirit and soul
Gives me the strength to achieve my goal.
You are in such a wonderful place,
Precious memories of you I'll embrace.
Roaming on those pastures so green,
Your shadow will always be seen.
Now in you I will always confide,

My secrets you protect with such pride.
Warning me about the antagonist,
You will always be my protagonist."

Solemn music played as the undertakers gently closed the lid of the coffin with pride and dignity. Family and friends cried passionately. I placed the palm of my hand on the closed coffin and cried with pain.

"Good-bye, dearest friend, good-bye," I whispered as she made her final journey to her new home, to her grave.

CHAPTER 9

The Immorality Act

An analogy can be drawn between the marital status of caste, religion, and social class and the Immorality Act of the apartheid system in South Africa. The Immorality Act was a strict code of conduct that prevented interracial affairs or marriages. By law no two races were allowed to marry. This act was first established in 1927 and amended in 1950. If a couple of different races was found dating, each person was given a five-year imprisonment. Mixed marriage was a taboo. This act was such a paradox since the Coloured population's existence was due to sexual relationships between White colonists and

Black slaves. The police were on the alert for mixed couples. Mixed couples were arrested, and, their underwear was used as forensic evidence to determine if they had sexual intercourse.

A peaceful demonstration by a mass group of Indians, Blacks, Coloureds and some Whites was held on West Street downtown. It was the main street of exclusively White-owned stores and restaurants. The demonstration calling for the end of the apartheid system and to free Nelson Mandela from prison was peaceful, a multiracial mass march. Riot police and law enforcement officers stood close by. With loudspeakers activists voiced their opinions, and the demonstrators cheered on the main street as well as all along Durban City Hall.

My mother was in the crowd, but with her group, the Business and Professional Women of South Africa. I went along with my group of university students. The demonstrators remained strategically nonviolent. White faces from the restaurants above peered down at us as if witnessing the heights of insanity. This was our only measure to facilitate our grievances. I marched with friends, and we held hands as we walked along. The group came to a standstill at city hall. We sat on the pavement to listen to speeches.

"Did you notice that person staring at you?" asked Cherry.

"No, where?" I laughed.

"To your right, a row in front of us," she said.

I looked over my right shoulder and spotted a blond-haired, blue-eyed person whose stares were like a dart aiming at a dartboard. I did not understand his glances, but they were piercing enough for me to acknowledge them. I shaded my eyes from the glaring, hot sun with the palm of my right hand and looked in his direction. It was the same White person I'd met while hiding from the riot police in the lecture auditorium. He waved and I waved back. I became prey to a host of emotions through this phenomenal experience. His glimpse seemed passionate, as if cupid were sending arrows in my direction. It was as if he were in search of me. I was intoxicated with the notion of such affection. Body language told me that this was a classic conception of love.

"I've seen him somewhere," said Cherry.

"In the lecture auditorium," I whispered.

"He is really handsome. Make your move," whispered Cherry.

"I do not even know his name. Plus, he is White, if you have not noticed," I giggled.

"He cannot take his eyes off you," she mischievously uttered.

I had no sense of what instantaneous true love symbolized, but my eyes beamed like crystals. I felt a volatile feeling in the heat. It was mushy, a feeling that I had not felt before. I did not know if he was watching me or I was watching him. But I knew for sure that I was observing him watching me. I saw him passing a note along the crowd, and I wondered what it was.

"It's for the one in the pink-and-white-striped top, just pass it along," he yelled out loudly.

A note was relayed through the crowd and landed in my hands.

"That's for you!" exclaimed a stranger.

"Thank you!"

I opened the note curiously. It read CALL ME, with his telephone number below. It was signed Piet. I was glad that I had finally discovered his name. Piet was a typical Afrikaner name, I thought to myself. I looked at him and with body language acknowledged his note. He winked with a warm smile and I smiled back, wondering if this could be a new chapter in my life. I blushed as Cherry teased me and Danny gave me a strange look.

It felt like a romantic attraction. I felt a passionate arrow strike my fragile heart, and it pierced deeply. It gave me an overwhelming desire and longing to be close to him. I was charmed by his presence and spellbound by the circumstances in which the relationship was growing. The attraction entered my eyes and penetrated my soul. It was instant gratification. I studied the handwriting on the piece of paper and then folded it and placed it in my jeans pocket. It was love at first glimpse. I felt intoxicated with such affection. I was not looking for my other half. To me it was just a classic conception of courtly love, in a modern setting. I was ravaged by the thought that someone showed interest in me in a circumstance where I least expected it.

The next speaker ascended the steps of city hall. He was a distinguished gentleman. He was White with dark blond hair, graying at the temples. He was dressed in an elegant gray designer suit with a burgundy tie. He was polished, with an air of distinction, dignity, and eminence.

"Amandla, amandla!" he chanted.

"Amandla, amandla, power to the people!" the crowd chanted after him.

"I am Mr. Jan, a lawyer with Jan and Company law firm. Today we are gathered here to ask our government to bring freedom to all people…"

He sounded like a distinguished scholar. His strong words penetrated through the crowd as he gave a remarkable speech.

"He looks identical to the boy who slipped you the note," said Cherry.

"You mean Piet. Yes, you are right. I recall at the demonstration on campus he told me that his father was a lawyer and he was a law student. Hmmm," I sighed.

"They have the same voice too!" exclaimed Cherry.

"Um, the same tone," I acknowledged.

The man spoke about human rights and human justice. He condemned the torture and beatings of political prisoners. He had strong words against those who used execution and brutality against such prisoners. He called for the end of the apartheid regime in South Africa. He singled out people who were responsible for the political terror that afflicted the entire population. He acknowledged that such political terror was aimed at a certain sector of the population.

"We have to reflect on the human rights violations, human rights abuses by insurgents of the police department and the government, that give rise to terrorist activities…"

"Well said," acknowledged Danny.

The crowd cheered on as the man spoke about longing for a free South Africa where all races could live together as one.

After the demonstration I hung out at the beach with a group of friends. The Durban beach was a popular hangout for all of us. It was a perfect, safe place where we could eat, drink, and chat. We were not equipped with our bathing suits, although we played along the water's edge at the Blue Lagoon. We were so engaged in conversation that we were struck by a huge wave and found ourselves submerged in the water up to our waists. I ran away from the water. I was so soaked that the dye from my dark blue jeans bled onto my pink-and-white top. We slept on the sand hoping that the hot sun would dry us up within seconds. It was almost as if the solitary wave had played a mischievous game with us. It did not take long for our clothes to dry on us, with the radiant South African sun smiling upon our tanned bodies.

When I got home that evening, I remembered the telephone number in my jeans pocket. I was so excited to call Piet. I picked up the receiver and blushed. When I took out the piece of paper, there was no number on it. The white piece of paper had turned blue. When that massive wave had hit, it washed out the telephone number. The blue dye from my jeans smudged the paper, erasing the number.

I ran to my room, disappointedly plopped on my bed, and began to cry. I knew that Piet must have been waiting for my call. Most boys had the three-day rule. If a girl did not call after three days, they knew that she was not into them. I had no way of reaching him. I wished that we had not gone to the beach after the demonstration.

Weeks passed and I did not see Piet. A group of friends and acquaintances on campus organized a camping trip to a beach in Transkei, called the Wild Coast. We looked forward to going away from Durban. We thought that it would be relaxing to get away from all the demonstrations in the city.

A group of ten girls boarded the train with our camping gear. We knew that it was going to be fun away from the city. Our parents said good-bye to us at the station. As the train traveled along the coast, we enjoyed the spectacular land and seaside. The scenery was simply breath taking. We passed beautiful green mountains and hills, dense with vegetation. We watched the huge waves break on the rocky beaches of the coast. We passed various farms where people generated their lively hoods, through a combination of livestock farming and crop farming. There was a cluster of beautiful huts along the way. They were Zulu huts on Zulu homesteads that revealed the anthropological disciplines of the Zulu tribes. The roofs were stacked with dried twigs, all placed in a precise umbrella formation. The bodies of the huts were made with brick and clay. They were painted in vibrant shades of red, yellow, blue, green, orange, and purple. The designs were so intricate and sophisticated, almost as if leaving room for interpretation.

Zulu women sat along the roads, engaging in the finest beadwork jewelry. They made the most exotic pieces and sold them at a reasonable price. They communicated loudly in their poetic speech, also known as Zulu, with the common click of the tongue between each word. The men sat isolated, carving wooden statues that revealed their artistic talents. The Wild Coast was a typical tourist industry. Little Zulu children ran around rolling car tires in role-play. Some stood at the roadside and along the beach selling bunches of freshly plucked fruit.

"Oh my God, I left my nail polish behind!" cried Lanelle.

"You are such a drama queen. Why do you need nail polish when we are going camping?" asked Amy.

"I figure we could meet some cute guys at the beach. Those beach boys," she laughed.

"And the drama begins," sighed Amy.

With a group of girls together, it was always lots of fun. However, tension did build up because of the clash of personalities. Lanelle was noted for being an attention seeker and very forward with boys, which angered most of the other girls. She was from a middle-class background with an unrealistic perception of the real world. She was always seeking attention. She came from a single-parent family but made dramatic moves on wealthy boys from the upper social class. She was a typical gold digger.

"You are looking down, what's wrong?" Melanie asked me.

"Oh, just admiring the beautiful scenery," I said, trying to show some enthusiasm.

Deep down inside I was sad to leave the city because I knew that I would not get a chance to bump into Piet. Furthermore, I knew that he would think that I was not interested in him and he'd move on to another girl. That was my loss. As I looked through the train window and admired the passing scenery, my mind was like a visual slide. I kept thinking about Piet admiring me at the demonstration. The part when he passed his telephone number to me, scribbled on a white piece of paper, played in my mind. In my thoughts, I rewound the incident several times, playing it over and over again in my mind until I fell into deep slumber, dreaming about him.

"Wake up, Kay! Wake up, Sleeping Beauty!" yelled the girls.

"Are we there already? Oh my God!" I said excitedly.

I had been in such a deep sleep that I hadn't realized the two hours of traveling had passed by.

We excitedly got off the train with our belongings. Lanelle had organized for us to stay at a convent. She belonged to a Catholic church, and she'd made arrangements with members from her church for us to camp at the convent, which was directly opposite the beach. It was also walking distance from the train station.

The convent was a Christian school for girls. It was run by a group of White nuns and a priest. Parents from Christian backgrounds sent their daughters to live at the convent, and the girls received their education from the nuns, who were teachers. The convent followed the same academic curriculum as public schools. However, discipline was strict, and the girls were required to do additional religious studies. On weekends and public holidays, the girls from the convent were allowed to return home for a vacation.

"Wow, this is such a beautiful building!" I exclaimed.

"Amazing, splendid," replied Amy.

"So mysterious and mystic," I sighed.

"Beautiful," chorused the others.

We stood for a while at the gates of St. Anthony's. A bright, beautiful brass plate at the gate read St. Anthony's Academy, a

RELIGIOUS SCHOOL FOR ALL GIRLS. It sparkled in the sun like a bar of gold. The building resembled a gigantic medieval castle, built in solid beige stone. It featured an enormous tower with a massive iron bell hanging from the top. It was impressive, unmarred by modern restoration. I felt as if I were stepping into another era. The weathered stone building accented a prefabricated fort. It was like a Roman castle, with intrinsic strength. It was a proud stonemason's work of art, showing professional craftsmanship. It was as if we had unveiled a cryptic or Gothic mansion in the middle of nowhere. I saw it as a perfect place for a spiritual or psychological experience.

That was such a vital moment in my life, when I discovered this castle with such archaeological interest. Lanelle rang the bell on the gate. The huge, impenetrable cast-iron gate looked as if it was for protection from a marauding army. It was like an exotic curtain made of cast iron. The beautiful convent building was visible through the bars of the gate.

"Good afternoon, goie middag," said a sweet White voice in both English and Afrikaans. She spoke through an intercom. "We are the girls from Durban," said Lanelle nervously.

"Darlings, I was expecting all of you. Hold on, give me a few minutes," replied the nun.

She could have just opened the gate for us, but she was courteous enough to come to the gate to welcome us. The huge wooden doors of the convent school opened with a screech. A tall, beautiful nun dressed all in white stood at the door. A long, traditional-style stone path led up to the gate. The paving itself was dazzling, a dramatic entrance that enhanced the exotic gardens around it. It was a harmonious setting.

As graceful as a bird in flight, the nun elegantly ran towards the gate. I felt as if I were in *The Sound of Music*. It was a picture-perfect scene. She glided towards us like an angel, all in white.

We were spellbound by her presence. It seemed as if she were moving in slow motion.

"Hello, darlings, I am Sister Meril," she smiled.

"Hello," we said nervously.

The gates opened in slow motion and Sister Meril stood there with the most sparkling blue eyes and her warm smile. She reached out and gave us a group hug. For a moment I did not feel as if I was in South Africa. We were away from the demonstrations in the city. Along the coast the atmosphere seemed so inviting and friendly.

"I have a room prepared for all of you," she softly said in a South-African British accent. "Dear me, dear me, indeed. You must be hungry and tired." Her voice came out like a tune. "Now, don't be afraid. Come along, girls." She summoned us to our dormitory, which was in the residential quarters.

Several White fathers or priests passed and politely greeted us with a bow. They then made the sign of the cross—*In the name of the father, the son, and the Holy Spirit*—and continued down the mysterious corridors. Several nuns passed us by, gave a friendly hello, and made their way towards the chapel. This had to be heaven on earth, I thought. The atmosphere was so quiet and so spiritual.

"We miss our girls on vacation, so I am glad to have you girls here," said Sister Meril with warmth and enthusiasm. "Do enjoy your stay at St. Anthony's."

We settled into our room with excitement. We arranged our sleeping bags on the bunk beds. Lanelle and Amy wanted to go to the beach for a stroll. The other girls just wanted to relax and explore the gardens around the convent.

"We are off to the beach!" yelled Amy excitedly.

"Do not forget, the nuns gave us a curfew. You should be back before it gets dark, around six o'clock to seven o'clock!" I yelled.

"Oh yeah!" said Amy as she gave me the middle finger with much attitude and disrespect.

We walked around the convent school, which was picturesque, mysterious, and fascinating. It seemed like a place for royalty and nobility. It was hidden in a remote area in the Wild Coast, Transkei, directly opposite a rocky beach. Walking around was so inspirational. It brought out the gentler and more romantic side of me. There must have been about one hundred twenty rooms. There was also a most beautiful cathedral. It was a majestic Gothic castle built over the centuries. Most of the rooms were used as classrooms, which never failed to impress us. I wondered if it had any myths or legends surrounding it. The winding corridors and elegant stone staircases were a brilliant example of Gothic architecture. The insides were well intact. It was also the official residence for many Catholic nuns and priests.

Several nuns passed us by. They were all White and very friendly. They allowed us to explore the convent without interfering. We walked to the east end to visit the same cathedral with the most fascinating contemporary architectural design. We could see the pride of great craftsmen in the most renowned architecture. I was simply spellbound by such ecclesiastical features, fit for royalty. Although most of us were Hindus and Muslims, with the exception of Lanelle, we knelt down and prayed since the atmosphere was so spiritual and silent.

We left the cathedral and walked into the atrium with its large, square cloisters. There was a series of lower chambers along a wide, arcaded passage that featured more dormitories, a refectory, and a massive library used by students and teachers. I realized that the massive mansion had a cruciform shape with an exotically defined axis. The façade of the west end was ornate. The huge monastic doors were richly decorated with sculpture, stone tracery, and marble. We walked down several arcades until we arrived at a tomb, which made us frantically run through corridors adorned with mosaics and marble friezes and huge stained glass windows. The complex arrangement of curving arcades on various levels led us into the most exotic gardens.

There were endless displays of spectacular arrangements of tulips and hybrid flowers in vibrant hues of red, yellow, purple, pink, and orange. The landscape was marvelous. The evergreen shrubs formed a fairy-tale maze. The botanical garden was extensive and breathtaking. I could not understand why Lanelle and Amy would want to go to the beach when the convent was so exotic. Besides, we saw the beach daily in Durban.

"Those girls are such attention seekers," said Melanie. "Look at what they are missing out on."

"They have more days to explore," I replied.

"I want to live here forever," she excitedly said.

"Become a nun and your dreams will come true," I sarcastically giggled.

We chatted with some nuns who gave us the history of the majestic place. When we returned to our dorm room, Amy and Lanelle were not there and it was past their curfew. The nuns did not check on us, so I guessed that they did not care. I knew the girls would have to secretly creep in so that the nuns would not notice.

At about ten o'clock that night the girls returned, excitement in their voices.

"We met some boys at the beach. Cute ones too," they uttered in chorus.

"Boys in such a remote area," I giggled in disbelief.

"Oh yes! We got carried away chatting. That's why we're late," said Lanelle.

We gathered around to hear more stories about the boys, but the girls seemed secretive and did not tell us all.

That night I could not fall asleep. Images of Piet and seeing him at the demonstration flashed through my mind. I still had regrets about losing his telephone number.

The next day Lanelle and Amy left early. They said that the boys were having a beach barbecue. They did not bother to invite any of us. The other girls began to gossip about them vindictively.

"Such whores," said Beverly.

"We are still having fun," I said to calm her down.

"Let's go to the beach too," said another.

"We've seen enough of clear waters, sandy shores, and spectacular views. Let's explore this massive castle!" I said with delight.

"Tonight, then," said another.

"This afternoon," I replied.

The rest of the girls got along well. We continued to explore the castle-like mansion. That afternoon we left the mansion gates and crossed over a narrow, quiet road. We walked through a short, bushy pathway and landed on the spectacular beach, with endless sandy shores and a spectacular rocky dunes. There were several huge tents pitched at the picnic and barbecue area. We walked along the impressive stretch of crystal-clean, sandy beach in the direction of the tents. The beach was quiet and almost private. We stood on the rocks and fed seagulls pieces of bread. It was different from our city beaches because we did not have so many rocks. The sand dunes, tidal flats, and lagoon added to our memorable experience.

"Hey, girls, two boys from the tent are walking in our direction!" exclaimed Melanie.

"Oh, just ignore them," said Beverly.

"Are they cute?" I asked.

"Don't know, the sun is in my eyes," said Melanie.

As the boys approached, they looked familiar to me.

"Hey, girls, would you like to join us?" one of them asked. "Two of your friends are already at our barbecue."

"You look familiar," I said.

"We go to the same university as all of you. We are also here to get away from the political demonstrations in the city," he said.

"Do you have a name?" I asked sarcastically.

"Sorry, I'm Anwar, and this is my friend Rob," he politely apologized.

Anwar was Indian and Rob was White. It was strange to see Indians and Whites hanging out together in this remote area. Knowing that they attended the same university as we did made us feel a little comfortable. We followed them to their barbecue party. Lanelle and Amy looked so comfortable, as if they had known the boys forever. I could see Lanelle's back. She was sitting on a rock next to a White boy. She had her hands through his hair in a flirtatious manner, obviously a romantic and sexual overture. Amy stood at the barbecue with another, holding his hand, subtly indicating an interest in a deeper relationship. Their verbal communication and body language spoke for itself.

"What a coquette," said Beverly.

"Shh! They can hear you," said Melanie.

"They move so fast," Beverly commented.

"Hey, it is not our business," I laughed.

Following the rules of social etiquette, the boys introduced themselves to us. They were very polite and sophisticated, which gave me the signal that we were safe. Amy walked away with the object of her sexual interest, as if we were going to steal him away from her. He was a good-looking, tall, and well-built Indian male. The other girls laughed at her body language. Lanelle and the White boy she was with did not even notice us. She continued to flirt with him intently.

I turned my back to them, and all the other girls stood around the barbecue. The boys were hospitable and generous. Chivalry was not dead. They honored our company. They followed all the moral and social codes of conduct, which made us feel welcome. We girls were just as courteous and respectful in return. We laughed and sang, and the conversation was bubbly and animated.

"Hey, Piet, you want a hot dog for you and your little lady?" Rob yelled out.

The name Piet pierced my heart with a thousand arrows. Shocked, I turned around. I stared into the deep blue eyes of Piet, and he returned my glance with the same amount of shock. We maintained eye contact for a while. I chose to remain silent and instantly turned back. I felt such personal rejection. He was with another girl. He gave me the silent treatment and the cold shoulder. I immediately felt insecure and depressed, with a sudden sense of social isolation. The moment was emotionally painful. My self-esteem was low. Although I was with a group of wonderful people, there was a missing ingredient. My emotions triggered intense anger, despair, and frustration in me. I thought that his aspirations for me were higher.

Humiliated, I felt tears fill my eyes. I could not control those tears.

"What's wrong?" asked Anwar.

"The smoke is getting into my eyes," I lied.

Before he could ask another question, I walked hastily away towards the water. I climbed up to the highest rock and sat there watching the waves break. Beverly followed me and perched herself upon the same rock.

"What's the matter?" she asked. "You were having so much of fun."

"Yes, until——" I stopped with rejected sensitivity.

I explained to Beverly about all my encounters with Piet, tracing every detail. She was not aware of my plight and listened enthusiastically. It hurt me that Lanelle was making her moves on him. That was so strange because he did not belong to me. I did not even know him well enough to react with such rejection. My heart played strange games with me, and I was reluctant to find a logical cognitive reasoning in such a controversial story. This was an ambiguous social encounter, and I was glad that I had my colleague Beverly close to me to share my story. My sense of rejection made me neurotic. It was difficult to bear. I did not know if I should go back to the group and flirt with the males to see Piet's reaction or just socially isolate myself from the group. I displayed such extreme behaviour when there was no intense romantic love between us. I yearned for Piet to return to me.

"You are just addicted to love," commented Beverly.

"Why is he ignoring me?" I asked, as if she was my psychiatrist.

"He most likely thought that you rejected him when you did not call him," she said, trying to make sense of the situation. "Maybe you should break the ice."

"Maybe I need time to think," I replied.

Beverly walked me back to the convent. I could not bear the feeling of rejection. I needed time to ponder the situation alone. Beverly left, returning to the beach, and I walked to the dorm. Halfway there, I stopped and walked down another arcade, which led me to the cathedral. I sat there alone on a pew and reflected on my delicate situation. I was in the perfect place at the perfect time. I felt an instant gratification. It was almost as if I heard a clear message from God. A smile came over me as I walked up to a candle, enthusiastically lit it, and prayed for peace of mind. I felt a warm feeling come over me. I recalled what Danny always told me, that if I do not have a ring on my finger, the boy does not belong to me. A nun entered. She smiled at me and proceeded to the altar. I looked at her and wondered what had motivated her to become a nun.

I freed myself from my obsessive thoughts. I regained an inner calmness and tranquility. I gained an inner sense of peace and freedom. I was not going to nurture any ill feelings or grievances. That note and glances from Piet were now bygones. I felt an epiphany come over me. A few more nuns came in; they looked at me with delight.

I ran back through all those corridors and arcades to my dorm. I took a quick shower, changed, and headed back to the beach. As I neared I could hear the loud music and laughter. I could feel the high energy. I was ready to love life and live large. The crackle of the campfire was part of the atmosphere. The sound of the guitar was uplifting.

"Hey, where have you been?" asked Melanie.

"Just a headache. Went back to the dorm, I feel better now," I replied.

Everyone was dancing, singing, and having fun. Amy and Lanelle were now part of the group. However, they still had their eyes on their chosen mates. I joined in the crazy dance, and I was ready to experience the joy of being at the beach party. Lanelle continued to flirt with Piet. She also seemed to flirt with the other boys, probably with the hope of making Piet jealous. I smiled at him as if I did not care and continued to entertain myself and be entertained by others.

The sun began to set. It lingered on the horizon. The disk of the sun illuminated the horizon in various shades of orange and red and lit up part of the sky. The ocean glittered like crystals. The tall palm trees were just a shadow overlooking the ocean, creating a looser and more romantic atmosphere. It made it easier for us to communicate. In no time everyone chattered amiably. I felt the sea breeze through my hair. The wonderful aroma of the barbecue stimulated my appetite. The situation was unique and exhilarating. I walked down to the shoreline to experience the thrill of being in the water during sunset. Fluffy, white waves broke on the shore. I dipped my feet into the warm water, which felt so soft and smooth with a salty smell. Slipping away during sunset gave me the most romantic and subdued feeling. It filled up my spirit and brightened my mood. I felt the water slip out, leaving wet sand between my toes.

Suddenly, I felt a tap on my shoulder and jumped with fright.

"It's only me," smiled Piet.

"Fancy seeing you alone. Where is your other half?" I sarcastically giggled.

"You mean Lanelle? She is not my other half. No romantic feeling. She just enjoys flirting—a bit of a drama queen," he giggled. He stared at me with glassy eyes and then asked, "Are you jealous?"

"Of course not! Are you crazy? Oh my God, what's wrong with you?" I stuttered.

He splashed me with water; I tried to run away and splashed him.

"I'll get you!" he yelled.

I ran along the water, and Piet grabbed me and took me into the warm, bubbly waves. We splashed each other like children fascinated by the ocean. He carried me up, as if he were going to throw me into the next massive wave. I held on tightly to him and begged him to let go. The waves rolled in like galloping white horses. They splashed all around us as if playing the same game. I felt a sense of pleasure and excitement. It was a perfect romantic ambience.

The wave rolled back, leaving us in the perfect embrace. We were immersed in each other's eyes for a long time without a spoken word. He leaned closer to me, and I willingly allowed him to. He placed the palms of his hands on both my cheeks and we enjoyed the closeness. I felt the awe of emotions and the butterflies in my stomach. Everything seemed to be moving in slow motion. I felt the magic of the first kiss take me over. I felt the touch of sensuality and comfort. Piet dropped his gaze, and I gave him a welcoming smile. He twined his arms around my neck and ran his fingers though my hair. He kissed me lightly on the forehead and gazed into my eyes. He gave me a peck on my lips, which was tender, romantic, and memorable. Gently he pushed my chin up, looked into my eyes, and softly and subtly whispered, "I love you." We then staged our very own kissing marathon that ultimately stole the night.

The sunset had vanished and the sky was pitch black. Thousands of green stars sparkled like emeralds in the sky, creating a new energy. The huge white waves were like neon lights rolling in the dark, illuminating the beach.

I had felt the physical attraction from the first time I had seen him. But that very moment I felt the spiritual and emotional connection. I was optimistic and happy. We both experienced love, a euphoric emotion. I felt an immediate palpable tingling sensation.

Another huge wave approached and swept us to shore, knocking us off our feet. Piet was on top of me, and I felt the magic power of love. I felt the seeds of passion as he continued to kiss me tenderly, gently, and then passionately. The chemistry between us was strong. We felt the elation and obsession of true love. The electric charge set the sand on fire, and there was no room between us.

"You did not call me," he whispered.

"It's a long story," I said and then explained why, still feeling the touch of his body over mine. I felt the adrenaline rush and gently moved his head towards mine, kissing him gently as if to apologize. Our hearts hammered as one. The loving feel of his muscular body comforted me.

The moon shone brightly like a spotlight over us as we felt the passionate love. I felt elated and in a romantic feeling of ecstasy. We kissed passionately. I wondered what such emotional chaos would lead to. There was a notion of intimacy and commitment. Being in his arms, I felt protected.

"Hey, there! What are you doing? Been looking for you." It was Lanelle's voice.

"What do you want?" asked Piet.

"What are you doing with this [bleep, bleep] bitch?" She uttered such profanities. "I want to talk with…with…with you!" she cried.

"Leave us alone—are you insane? Watch your foul language, I am in the presence of a fine lady!" yelled Piet.

He gently picked me up from the sand and lightly embraced me with such tenderness.

"I'm sorry," he apologized.

"She's just a loose cannon," I comforted him. "That's the way she always acts, the centre of attraction, drama queen," I continued.

To avoid any further confrontation, we strolled back to the campsite. The others were sitting around a campfire toasting marshmallows. I knew that I had found unconditional love. Piet was patient, kind, and compassionate.

Beverly reminded us that it was late and we had a curfew. In fact, it was past our curfew. We had to sneak back into the convent without the nuns knowing. All the girls got up to leave. Piet insisted that he walk back with me.

"But what if the nuns see you, what will they think?" I asked.

"We'll have to duck and dive," he laughed.

We walked through the bushy pathway and silently, like rodents, ran across the narrow road. We did not enter through the front gate because the nuns were bound to see us. We crept through the side. There was a small, wooden arched door that was slightly ajar. It led through the main courtyard. The girls entered through the door and I was the last one. Piet grabbed me and hugged me. He kissed me passionately.

"Sleep tight, I'll miss you," he whispered.

"Come on, Kay!" urged Melanie.

I ran in, closing the door behind. We went through the first arcade like mice in the dark. We heard the footsteps of nuns approaching and hid behind a huge pillar in a notch-like crevice. The nuns passed us as we froze in the huge notch. They walked silently down the arcade and then down another until we heard a huge door creak open and then shut.

"That was a close call," uttered Melanie.

"Quiet, they may hear us," I whispered.

We made our way back to the dorm. Like cats, we slowly walked along the walls. I walked up to the dorm balcony and peered out. Piet was still standing at the small wooden door. I waved and he threw a kiss. I read the words on his lips as he mouthed, "See you tomorrow!" He gazed at me, and I knew that he was also in love. I closed the balcony window as I watched Piet disappear into the quiet night.

CHAPTER 10

Forbidden Love

The next morning I woke up beaming with excitement. However, I felt as if I had taken a bite from the forbidden apple in the Garden of Eden. The relationship between Piet and me was forbidden. It was against the Immorality Act of the apartheid era in South Africa, two races were not allowed to enter into a romantic relationship. It made matters even worst if the couple belonged to the White and non-White race. I'd entered into troubled waters. I could not understand why love needed any barriers. To me love was colourblind.

All the girls woke up late. We hastened to the beach that afternoon, excited and enthused. Opening the gates of the convent was like opening the gates of heaven because I felt so lighthearted and in love. When I stepped onto the beaming, hot sand, Piet spotted me and ran towards me. He lifted me up, twirled me around, and passionately kissed me.

"I could not wait to see you," he uttered excitedly.

"That makes two of us," I whispered.

The boys and girls got together, playing volleyball and soccer on the beach. Others swam and some surfed. Piet and I spent the entire day just sitting on the beach talking. He told me all about his past, and I told him all about mine. The conversation flowed easily and confidently. We did not socialize with others because we were so interested in getting to know each other, with such compassion. Our romantic passion did not cease.

That night we gathered around the campfire. It was another starry night. We held long skewers over the flame and cooked hot dogs. We also toasted marshmallows. It was the perfect venue for conversation, singing, and storytelling. The evening was perfect. We played games and socialized with our new friends. It was a relaxing and exotic experience. Through storytelling we discovered surprising facts about each one's past and personality. This helped us bond with each other. We tested our acting skills, which identified Rob as the clown in the group. Soft music played in the background as the stars gazed upon us. It was a picture-perfect night.

"Do you hear voices?" asked Melanie.

"Just your imagination," laughed Bob.

"Oh, I hear it too," acknowledged Anwar.

Piet let go of my hand. Everyone stared in the direction of the voices. We thought that it was just people walking along the dark shores of the beach. Suddenly, out of the blue, appeared a gang of white adult males. There must have been about five of them, and they looked like thugs. We were terrorized by this group of men who were violating our privacy. I felt traumatized.

"What are you White boys doing with these coolies at the beach?" asked a heavily built one as he pushed Rob aside.

We froze and nobody said a word. Fear and panic took over instantly. The men were armed with weapons and obviously there to torment us.

"Is that your girlfriend, dude?" asked one, pointing at Piet and I. Without hesitation Anwar jumped right next to me and uttered nervously.

"She is my girlfriend—girl!"

"Oh, so you are the smart one, coolie," he said and slapped Anwar across the face.

We were in a remote location and there was no one around to help. The men were big, with Harley Davidson leather jackets. They asserted that they were cops. However, to me they resembled the Hell's Angels motorcycle gang. They looked like misfits and a malcontent group. One turned around and I spotted the Hell's Angels medal on his jacket and a patch denoting his rank. All five of them were six feet tall or more, in their late thirties and forties. They had long, blond, wavy hair in ponytails and long blond beards. What scared me most were the tattoos all over their arms and the fierce-looking silver rings on their fingers. All Hell's Angels were White-supremacist, nationalist, and racist. One waved his hatchet, and I wondered if we were going to be hacked to death. Most of these supremacists had training from the South African police. Therefore, they were skilled at self-defense.

"We belong to the Afrikaner Weerstandsbeweging! Yes, the Afrikaner Resistance Movement!" yelled one. His loud voice echoed like thunder through the peaceful night.

"Die wit man!" he yelled in Afrikaans. "What is jou naam?" (The White man. What is your name?)

"Piet!" Piet answered, trembling.

"You like the coolies, neh?" he yelled at Piet in a strong Afrikaans accent.

"I just met them at the beach, while Rob and I were fishing," he said.

If they knew that Rob and Piet were part of the group, that would have caused more violence. Piet was intelligent enough to distract them. I knew that the Afrikaner Weerstandsbeweging chief, Eugène Terre Blanche, had threatened civil war if the apartheid system was dismantled. Most of his followers were Afrikaners who lived on the farms. They believed that the end of the apartheid system meant surrendering to communism. They were brutal and ruthless in their tactics. They orchestrated many assassination attempts on the lives of political activists.

The other three Hell's Angels waved their pipes, pangas (machetes), and hatchets as the leader spoke in Afrikaans to Piet and Rob. Many had been murdered amid all the racial controversy, and this encounter at the beach threatened our existence. We were terrified.

I felt the tension amongst our group. Lanelle and Amy showed their softer sides as they began to cry.

"We need a White earth!" yelled another in a strong Afrikaner accent. "No Black rule or destruction of the Afrikaner people!"

His thunderous voice echoed with passion and made my heart beat faster. He roared like a lion, with aggressive gestures and nonsensical words.

"You coolies are a racist menace!" he barked.

"Your plight is in my White hands," another said in a husky whisper.

"I will throw all of you into the Indian Ocean so you can swim back to India!" joked another.

"The AWB will seize power by force. We have political thunder. We will continue to preach about our supremacies," gestured another, as if he were drafting constitutional negotiations with us.

We were still frozen by their antics. We'd gotten away from the demonstrations in the city to enjoy a peaceful vacation. On this remote beach, now we had to encounter these White Boer supremacists. We had to bow to them in order to save our lives. It seemed like death was on our doorstep. I knew that the AWB's politics had been ineffectual because South Africa and its people were ready for change.

Another two boys in our group scuffled with them in a heated confrontation. Anwar tried to stop it. I wondered if they had heard us singing rival anthems. We were starkly divided along racial lines. We had to maintain our dignity for the sake of survival. Two hours had gone by and I was exhausted.

We could not allow any scuffle to spiral out of control. I wondered about the nuns in the convent. I thought about the cathedral. I prayed in my mind that the supremacists would set us free, alive.

The tension grew as two more approached. To make matters worse, they were intoxicated. When they saw that we were a group of Indians, they began to sing an Afrikaner folk song in their drunken state.

> "Bobbejaan klim die berg
> So haastig en so lustig
> Bobbejaan klim die berg
> Om die coolies te verergevang
> Hooraa vir die jollie bobbejaan!"

I had learned that Afrikaner folk song at school when I'd first learned Afrikaans—my second language, English being my first. Those intoxicated supremacists had twisted the words to the folk song. Their interpretation meant the baboon climbs the mountain to catch the Indians. They referred to us as coolies.

Since it was an isolated area and the AWB were here, I knew that there must be a farming community close by and we were vulnerable to violent attacks. The AWB were similar to the Ku Klux Klan because they believed in White supremacy and White nationalism and were anti-immigration. They wanted White supremacy by threat and violence. The KKK wanted to purify American politics. In the same way, the AWB wanted a purification of South African politics.

When I noticed Piet with a bloody nose, I realized that the confrontation was going to be brutal. Tears streamed down my face, and I prayed that someone would come along and save us. The two intoxicated Hell's Angels summoned the other five. It seemed as if they needed to go somewhere.

"We will be back in the morning to kill all of you! Did you hear that?" one of them yelled at us.

"Yes, sir!" cried Lanelle.

"Wipe that smile off your face!" he yelled at Anwar, throwing a handkerchief at him.

Anwar pretended to wipe off the smile. I wondered if the nuns had given us a curfew because they knew the AWB was in the area. I regretted that we hadn't listened to them. After threatening us repeatedly, the Hell's Angels left. Hurriedly, we said good-bye to the boys. We planned to return the next morning to Durban. We were afraid the Hell's Angels would be back. We exchanged numbers with the boys and vowed to keep in touch, when we got back. We'd planned a three-week vacation, but we had to cut it short because of the dangers that were ahead.

I pleaded for Piet to allow us to walk back to the convent alone, but he insisted that he needed to see us there safely. A few of the boys walked us back as well. This time it seemed a little safer because it was just past midnight. We figured that the nuns must be asleep. The wooden gate was locked. That scared us because we knew that the nuns had locked it. I wondered if they had suspected we were using it to sneak out. The boys helped us jump over the wall at the gardens. One by one we plucked up the courage to jump over.

Piet gave me a tight hug. I felt the blood from his nose smear on my top.

"I will call you when we get back to Durban," he whispered.

"Sure, this time we will keep in touch," I nervously uttered.

The girls and I crept through all the arcades, past the cathedral, and into our dorm. The next morning we went down to the nuns' headquarters to say thank you and good-bye. They were surprised that we were leaving so soon.

"We expected that you would stay for another two weeks. What's the rush?" asked Sister Meril.

"Some girls are missing home!" exclaimed Lanelle.

"Please visit us soon. All of you are such wonderful children of God!" exclaimed sister Meril warmly and with a loving smile.

We could not take the risk of staying any longer. After bidding farewell to all the nuns, we made our way to the train station. The journey back to the city was so exciting that it went by quickly.

In Durban, Piet and I got comfortable in a cozy long-term relationship. His parents had bought him a luxurious condominium along the beach. Our friend Anwar posed as my boyfriend in public to divert attention away from Piet and me. It worked really well, and nobody suspected that we were dating. I do not believe that we were alone in our ordeal. There were mixed couples in South Africa who were in the same boat. We refused to succumb to the dictates of the Immorality Act. Therefore, Piet and I found ourselves anchored in the sanctuary of his condominium because we could not be seen together in public. Colonial racism had destroyed our human dignity.

Anwar always accompanied me to Piet's home. We held hands to divert the neighbors' attention. On one occasion, after Anwar had left, there was a knock at the door.

"Don't open it," I whispered fearfully.

"It's only Anwar, he left his keys on the table," laughed Piet.

"Oh, I see them," I calmly responded.

"Hi!" Piet exclaimed as he opened the door.

My body was like an anxiety machine as I spotted Mr. Jan, Piet's father, at the door.

"I was not expecting you, Dad," said Piet nervously.

"I was in the neighbourhood, and I thought that I would drop in to take you out for lunch," he said. "What's wrong? You sound nervous."

I looked into the eyes of Mr. Jan. He walked in like a hunter at daybreak. The naked truth of our relationship was immediately revealed. I felt the psychological trauma. The agonizing presence of his father moved me.

"Sorry, am I intruding?" he politely asked.

"Dad, this is Kay, my friend," said Piet.

"Friend?" replied his dad with one raised eyebrow. "A friend, indeed!" he continued with a smirk on his face.

We all gave a nervous laugh. The cat was out of the bag. Mr. Jan was not duped. He ordered takeout rather than going out for dinner. We spoke about our meeting, and Mr. Jan listened attentively, stopping to give us meaningful advice. Our safety was paramount. Instead of harping on the situation, he gave us all of his moral support.

Months passed and I noticed that Piet's neighbor always gave Anwar and me a curious look when we arrived. She seemed to be interested in all the neighbors' daily lives. She tried to befriend me, but I kept my distance. We lied to her that we were all at the same university, working on group assignments. Several times when we left Piet's flat, we spotted her close to the door and wondered if she'd been listening in on our conversations. She was one of those Whites who presented a facade, as if she was so democratic. Deep down we knew that she was just superficial. Her expression showed that she was a White supremacist. Conventional wisdom dictated that I should be friendly towards her, yet skeptical about revealing too much.

My parents did not know about my relationship, but they met Piet on several occasions and were impressed by his poise and personality. However, I believed that parental intuition must have told them that it was more than a friendship. They did not pry into my friendships and avoided the topic.

Months passed by and Piet and I reflected on a realistic commitment. We dreamed about being together as a couple, some day when the apartheid system was abolished. Our future was a mystery. Our past was unforgettable history. We lived with a combination of fearless creative energy and an increasing sense of paranoia. We were figuratively exiled from the mainstream public life in South Africa. Many young couples spent time hand in hand, strolling along the beach. The apartheid system engineered the romantic relationship between Piet and me. Our love story was governed by South African politics in the early 1980s. Our love was subject to dire oppression.

"Let's have a romantic picnic!" exclaimed Piet one day.

"Are you crazy, in the eyes of public scrutiny?" I cried.

"No, we can stage our very own picnic in my flat," he romantically whispered.

"Sounds good," I whispered back.

"This weekend, then."

"Uh-huh," I said with desire and passion.

I told my parents that I was going on a picnic and then camping with friends. They trusted me and acknowledged that I would behave discreetly. It was the first time that I was going to spend the night at Piet's condominium, and I was so thrilled. We had to form our own innovative ideas to add excitement to our crossracial relationship. The public, friends, and relatives were not present to render opinions and judgment. This gave us the freedom to express our passion behind closed doors. Our love was forbidden under racial pretext. It was such absurd drama. We found humor in such an absurd political system. We laughed about our children being zebras, with a combination of brown and white stripes. Our relationship was not morally justified, yet it was romantically motivated. We were the oppressed in a heartless political regime.

We improvised our romantic picnic in the living room. Piet opened the curtains and exposed the starry sky. The moon shone through the window, illuminating the room and adding its magical touch. The ocean breeze created a perfect romantic atmosphere. We laid a dried grass mat on the floor and filled it with snacks, seafood, chocolates, and fruit. Two wine glasses stood side by side, glistening in the moonlight. All our hopes and fears about the future were erased from our minds as we enjoyed our intimate picnic. We spoke about our biracial children. We wondered if they would be intrigued by our love story.

I'd written a romantic poem for Piet, which I'd laminated and framed. Tears of joy streamed down his red cheeks as I read the words to him:

We stubbornly reject the immorality law,
Our love so passionate, realistic, and raw,
A love so aesthetically pleasing
That authentic oppression is just teasing.
In the light of the apartheid political rule,
Our love is denied by a political fool.
Like rodents we sneak out in the night,
At day we demonstrate in a democratic fight.
Our children would be the forbidden fruit,
They would be intrigued by the truth.
Freedom curtailed to the boundaries of this flat,
Tired of hiding my face under this hat.
Engaged in passionate, illicit, interracial sex,
To the government it is considered to be vex.
A day at the beach our passion grew,
Our love story mixed in a political stew.
Apartheid government entered our private life,
Preventing me from becoming your wife.
Now we are subjected to dire punishment,
Immorality Act of an apartheid government.
They decide whom you should love;
God witnesses our passion from above.
Our true love engineered to be blind,
A romance like ours is so hard to find.
Colonists brought in South African oppression,
How can I remove such psychological depression?
The Afrikaner slept with the laborer's wife,
The Coloured community is visible and rife.

An Era of Error

Love across race is a forbidden subject.
Our hearts beat as one like a passionate object.
Values placed by the evil apartheid era
Declare our love a passionate error.
As a White you become the antagonist,
As a non-White I became the protagonist.
As a South African of Indian descent,
Stringent apartheid laws we try to bend.
Falling deeply in love with another race,
The Immorality Act is such a disgrace.
Our love is forced to live in such exile,
The apartheid laws are repulsive and vile.
The Immorality Act we are bound to cheat,
A law that we would someday defeat.
Hopelessly, I declare my love for you,
Someday we will be able to say, "I do."
We will witness this law being repealed,
Several times we have ardently appealed.
Our love has crossed the colour line,
Now and forever you would be mine.
A law designed to maintain racial purity
Of White South Africans and their security.
Intolerant and conservative atmosphere prevails,
An intense love story like this never fails.
Will we survive the apartheid incarceration,
Refusing to succumb to such devastation?
Enveloping us with feelings of guilt,
The way the apartheid structure was built.
We swear that we will never, ever part,
Your love is entrenched deep in my heart.
Your presence makes my heart beat so fast,
It is the type of love that will last.

Someday you will be part of my life,
The day that I swear to be your wife.
Together we will live and grow old,
A romantic story that needs to be told.
Let's make a toast to our unconditional love
As God witnesses patiently from above.

It was the most beautiful night of passionate romance and intense communication. Piet seemed nervous and anxious to have dessert.

"I bought your favourite cheesecake," he said excitedly.

"Sounds fantastic, but I have no room for dessert," I pleaded.

He brought out the cheesecake on a fancy platter of gold and silver. It was a heart-shaped cake filled with edible gold beads. He placed it in front of me, and in the middle of the cake in black licorice icing, it read WILL YOU MARRY ME? Piet knelt down and looked at me like a puppy. He slipped a ring on my finger; its diamond sparkled. I wanted to seize that moment and make it last forever.

"Yes, I will!" I cried out.

"Thank you!" he politely exclaimed.

We took that opportunity to seal our engagement with a passionate kiss. We spoke about our future. If the Immorality Act was not repealed, we had no choice but to immigrate to another country. We had to make a choice to secure our future together.

That night we passionately cuddled in bed and fell off to sleep, feeling the warmth of each other's bodies.

"Sweet dreams," said Piet.

"Sleep tight," I whispered and we fell into deep slumber.

In the middle of the night, there was a knock on the door. We pretended not to hear it. The knock grew more violent. We knew that it was going to wake up the neighbours.

"I wonder who it is?" said Piet.

"Could be an emergency," I nervously replied.

"Open up or we will break this door!" came the thunderous roar.

"Hold on!" said Piet as he put on his robe.

In barged four South African policemen with obnoxious attitudes.

"So the neighbours were right!" yelled one.

"What hanky-panky is going on here?" yelled another.

"Put on your clothes, you *bleep, bleep, bleep*," he yelled.

A romantic night had come to a devastating end. Piet pleaded for them to be gentle with me.

"The both of you have violated the conditions of the Immorality Act. You are under arrest. You have the right to remain silent until you contact your lawyer," one of the policemen commanded with a strong Afrikaner accent.

We did remain silent as we suffered indignity. We were escorted to the political detention centre. We were stripped of all our belongings and escorted to the interrogation and torture chamber. God was the only witness to our faith. Piet was whiplashed with a sjambok and kicked by an interrogation officer who uttered vulgar profanities as he commanded him to move along. I had to cope with seeing them torture him in front of me. The violent slamming of several cell doors echoed through the building. I feared solitary confinement and was tormented by thoughts of death.

The impromptu interrogation began, and I feared the horrendous mental torture. Our human rights were violated as the interrogation storm began.

"Are you aware of the Immorality Act?" commanded the police officer.

"Yes, sir!" cried Piet.

"Then why did you enter into an interracial relationship, knowing that it is against the law, seun, boy?" he roared in both Afrikaans and English.

"I fell in love, sir." Piet sounded nervous.

"In love—love with a coolie," the officer said angrily.

His voice was like an earthquake. His temper measured nine on the Richter scale.

He lifted up his sjambok, the Zulu whip, and lashed Piet several times on his back. The sound of the whip was like the howling wind. I felt the pain of the whip on Piet's body. The sight of such corporal punishment made me dizzy. Blood oozed out of Piet's wounds, and he begged them to stop.

"Please, stop! Stop, stop!" I cried, vomiting at the sight of the blood.

Another officer slapped me across the face with such force that I felt a hot sensation around my nasal passages. Warm blood dripped onto the floor. I tried to get my mind off it by observing the cockroach-infested window ledges. Piet was handcuffed behind his back. The interrogation and torture continued.

The police officer bludgeoned Piet's head against the wall, kicking him at the same time.

"You have so many White girls out there. South Africa is your paradise. Yes, the White man's paradise, and you chose to deny our government, our laws. Speak up boy…!" he commanded.

"Sorry Soooory," was all Piet could say as he was moving in and out of consciousness.

"Stop please," I gave a bone-chilling cry.

"I will castrate him in front of you, if you do not stop girl," he threatened waving the sjambok at me.

Inflicting physical harm was not as severe as the psychological devastation. It seemed as if we were interrogated and tortured for days. My heart felt like a ticking bomb ready to explode. The room was cold and bleak. The officer's violent commands echoed through the room. His words came out like bullets, bouncing off the cold cement walls. Observing Piet was like watching a blood-curdling horror movie.

I decided to take a vow of silence, since each time I begged them to stop, it only provoked them to lash out at Piet. Two interrogators jostled him. His arms were bruised. He had big blue marks the size of tennis balls on several parts of his body. Their interrogation techniques were appalling.

I thought about Piet's parents. He was their only son, and his parents spoiled him to death. They gave him all their attention and unconditional love. I could imagine their faces if they saw Piet in this condition. For a moment I felt responsible for placing him in such circumstances. I blamed myself. I should not have allowed him to pursue a love relationship with me. I wanted to hold him and hug him. I wanted to tell him that I was sorry. I wondered if his parents would be angry with me for putting him through such torment. I wished that I were in his shoes, taking the beating for him.

A loud siren went off, causing me to jump out of my skin. The police officers exited the room. They slammed the door behind them in frustration. I jumped at the sound. I heard the key in the door and knew we were locked in. As their loud voices faded in the distance, I plucked up the courage to move close to Piet. He was on the floor in the fetal position.

"Piet!" I whispered. "Are you all right?"

He did not answer me. His naked body trembled. His lips quivered. He was as pale as a ghost.

"Piet…Piet…Piet…answer me!" I cried hysterically. "I am so sorry, Piet. Please forgive me. Piet, promise that you will forgive me!" My tears were uncontrollable.

A big, thick lump formed in my throat as I cried out his name several times. I began to shiver, and the loud sobs came out like hiccups. My throat ached. I felt the mucous run out of my nose. I felt like a child being severely punished.

Piet continued to shake. He looked up at me and rolled his eyes. He then stared at me in a daze. I was so accustomed to him giving me a romantic look. At that moment he did not even recognize me.

"Be strong for your parents, Piet. Hang in there. They will be so devastated to see you in this condition!" I cried hopelessly.

I continued to talk to Piet, although he did not reply. I knew that he did not have the energy to reply. I wished that he'd heard every word that I said because they'd come directly from my heart.

"Someday soon it is going to be fine, Piet. We will leave this country, the country of our birth, and travel abroad. We will be married and have several children. We will protect them from evil and not let them experience such torture. We will be fine, Piet, fine. Comfortable!" I sobbed.

Piet did not say a word. I saw a tear streak down his bloody face. I perceived that he had heard me. The tear formed a stream down his face, washing away the blood from its path.

My body ached as I bent down and kissed Piet lightly on his forehead. His body shivered. I leaned over him just to give him some body heat. It seemed to help him. I stroked his arms to let him know that it was all right. I cuddled him like a puppy. I knew that he needed medical attention. His parents had pampered Piet all those years, and sustaining such injuries must have been a shock to him. Tears streamed down my cheeks as I continued to talk to Piet to help him maintain his sanity. It bothered me that he did not move or respond. He was in a severe state of shock.

To get my mind off the situation, I softly ran my fingers through his silky blond hair and thought about our romantic past.

"Oh, Piet, do not forget the way we were!" I cried.

The words "the way we were" sparked memories of the song by Barbra Streisand, and I softly sang the lyrics to Piet as tears continued to flow down my cheeks.

Memories light the corners of my mind,

As I sang I recalled when Piet and I had walked along the beach near the convent on that starry, moonlit night. We'd splashed in the warm waters of the ocean as the huge, white, fluffy waves broke in. I thought about our first romantic touch. Then my thoughts moved on to our first romantic kiss. The sand had filtered through our toes and the water had retreated into the ocean, only to come back with full force and surround us, as if it were sealing our love. The memories moved through my mind as the words of "The Way We Were" escaped my lips.

I could not imagine how something that felt so right could be so wrong. When I stopped I felt Piet move. I looked down at him, and he slurred the words "I love you" with great effort. That was a miracle, as if his spirit conveyed the message.

He closed his eyes and rested his head upon my knee. I looked down at him in shock. The words of the song evoked sadness in me, yet they portrayed happy memories. That was an oxymoron. It was a paradox that a sad song could convey such happy memories. Singing those lyrics prevented me from becoming depressed. It helped me express my feelings for Piet and to show him how important our first meeting was. The lyrics of the song sailed through my mind over and over again. The vision moved in front of me, evoking such bittersweet emotions. The auditory nerve in my brain's centre sparked such deep-rooted emotions.

Piet and I were locked in a cold, grey cell, in social isolation. We were estranged from our family and friends. I had to break away from the chains of alienation by rewinding my thoughts to my romantic past. Music helped me express my human condition. It also helped Piet think about his existence in the vicious face of death.

Metaphorically, I was a jumbo shrimp. My presence around Piet was big; however, physically, I was petite. The notion of being powerless made me feel alienated. However, my emotions were deeply embedded in the present moment. Intrinsically, I felt a sense of satisfaction being with Piet. I thought that this might be our last time together, and I enjoyed every moment with passion. I repeatedly sang "The Way We Were," my voice singing Barbra Streisand, filling the cell with memories of Piet and me. Memories of love.

Like a tsunami wave, the police officers rolled in. I could hear their loud, thunderous voices echoing in the distance, in the narrow, long hallway. I knew that we were going to be bombarded with questions once more.

Despite the pain, I jumped up with fear. I ran back to my chair and pretended to be asleep. I peeped at Piet; the sound of their obnoxious voices made him tremble. The cell door key seemed to rattle and echoed through the room. The door was pushed open with force and aggression.

"Yes, Sleeping Beauty, you enjoyed your time alone with your lover," laughed the officer with a sarcastic tone.

"You are allowed one phone call," said another.

Piet's body shook rapidly, instigated by the tone of their voices. His shaking was uncontrollable. It seemed as if he was having a seizure. He displayed all symptoms of convulsions. I wonder why we were allowed a call after all the interrogation. I was not familiar with my legal rights.

"This is a medical emergency," said the giant-like police officer.

"Yes!" replied the other urgently.

Piet's eyes began to roll up, and he lost consciousness.

"You killed him, you [*bleep, bleep*] murderers, you killed him!" I gave a gut-wrenching yell.

I thought it was unusual that they did not respond to me. I saw fear come over their faces, which turned deep shades of red. It was a heart-rending moment. I cringed as I saw the paramedics barge in. I felt pangs of anguish and intense grief. One paramedic felt Piet's pulse and then looked up at me in a truly piteous manner.

The room turned cold and a biblical illusion of angelic white light circled the room. The overpowering presence of death pervaded my body. An intense feeling took over. In the presence of death, I stood at ease. An illuminated image of Piet swiftly glided through the room. He was dressed in white satin. I was gripped by his presence as I sang the song of life. It was a terrible presence that hovered above me. Yet I felt a sense of protection. The threshold of death surrounded me. I felt as if I were in another dimension. Piet summoned me to go with him.

I reached out to touch him. He slipped through my fragile fingers and drifted away. His soul stayed back to conspire with me. Intuition told me that Piet had passed away. My heart was as heavy as lead. My voice could not come out. My world began to spin in slow motion. I collapsed with grief and exhaustion.

The morticians arrived in thirty minutes. The policemen and interrogating officers forgot about me, as if I were a sheer ghost. In a trance I watched as they lifted Piet's body and placed it into a body bag. A cold, eerie feeling came over my body. I felt someone touch my shoulder and turned around in a coherent manner to find nobody there. I looked up to the ceiling and saw the spiritual vision of Piet, restless and anxious, looking down upon his limp body. His face glowed, and I could feel his presence. It was as if he intended to pray for his dead body on the ground. He stared at me, emotionless, and I felt a telepathic message enter my mind: *Sorry to leave you. I will guard and protect you forever!*

Those visions were so vivid. It was my unconscious talking to me, helping me set aside my ego and receive self-knowledge. It was not a hallucination; I saw the image of Piet based on the reality of my psyche. Piet existed in a different dimension. It was a visible reality to me. I felt the deluge of Piet's spirit pass through the cell. The round, white, enamel light shade fell to the ground with an enormous crash, sending pieces of glass flying through the air. The police officers ran out of the room in intense fear.

The morticians removed Piet's body in the body bag. I sat alone in the icy cold room. I was a forgotten soul, haunted by Piet's ghostly entity. I felt mystical sensations, followed by a feeling of deep space. I saw a bright light, and I felt as if I were hovering between life and death. It was as if Piet wanted me to go with him. I felt a void in my life. It was hard to accept the fact that Piet was gone. I could not dismiss the spiritual image of Piet. He wanted me to explore the realms beyond my physical existence. My deep-seated pain changed into spiritual wisdom as I closed my eyes with exhaustion.

Hours could have passed by, and I felt a tap on my shoulder. I woke up with a fright as I saw an older vision of Piet in front of me. I tried to focus. I shook with fear.

"It's me, Mr. Jan, Piet's dad." His calm voice was like music to my ears.

I did not respond. His eyes were puffy, swollen, and red from crying. His eyelids were swollen and wrinkled. I felt shock, numbness, and emptiness. He gently helped me to my feet. He hugged me and cried under the traumatic circumstances. It was the first time I'd seen a grown man cry with such pain. I instantly knew that I was not alone. Both of us exhibited the same extreme reaction as we hugged with compassion, sharing a common loss.

"He is gone, gone, gone!" sobbed Piet's father.

"Gone, gone," I repeated bitterly.

"Oh, God! I can't believe, my only son is gone, never to return." His sobbing grew stronger.

"He is gone," I repeated, feeling worthless.

He held onto me tightly to acknowledge his loss. I could not find any survival mechanism. Grief brought about physical, emotional, and cognitive changes in my body. I hung onto Mr. Jan as if forming a new attachment behaviour in an attempt to reinstate the relationship I shared with Piet. A warden led us out of the detention centre.

In the parking lot were all Piet's family, relatives, and friends. Amongst them I spotted my family members. The sobbing grew louder as the crowd in front of the detention centre echoed our cries. The atmosphere was filled with sadness, sorrow, fatigue, depression, anger, anxiety, and a sense of hope. Despite being in the company of so many people, I felt intense loneliness and isolation, which became overwhelming. The physical sensation of grief elicited disturbing emotions with family and friends.

A frail White woman came forth and hugged me, sobbing.

"My Piet is gone, my son is gone. Why? How? What did he say? What were his last words? Did he die suffering?" Piet's mother was in a deep state of depression.

Mrs. Jan's crying evoked intrusive thoughts of how Piet died. This impeded my ability to function. So intense was my grief that I lost consciousness in the parking lot, surrounded by loved ones.

I spent the next few days at the hospital trying to accept the reality of my loss. Denial became my enemy. I denied the fact that Piet was dead. Images of him flashed constantly through my mind, which was also filled with painful thoughts, and I could not find a simple strategy to cope with such depression and grief. I had to rediscover my own sense of self and identity.

I had to change the dynamics of my environment to cope with my grief. Moving to a new city meant emotional relocation. The words of Piet's father rang constantly through my mind: "Piet died fighting to dismantle the apartheid regime in South Africa. Piet is the real hero. He fought for freedom. Freedom came to him in death. It is time that racial discrimination dies for new relations to exist."

Mourning complicated my life and distorted my visions of the future. Grief followed me like a shadow. I explored pleasant memories of Piet as a means to facilitate a resolution to end my grief. My friends Beverly and Melanie walked into the hospital ward with mixed emotions; they were sad at the death of Piet yet happy to see me.

"I do not know if you are ready for this, but I have the moving speech taped from Piet's funeral," said Melanie, crying.

"The doctor felt that I was not ready to attend due to my failing emotional state," I sobbed.

"Maybe you are not ready to hear it now," said Beverly.

"I need some sort of closure to remind me that Piet has really passed on. I constantly see images of him still being alive," I sobbed.

"It was an eventful funeral packed with well-wishers who did not even know Piet," said Melanie.

"I know that he is smiling from above," I said.

"Ready to listen?" asked Beverly.

"Ever ready!" I exclaimed.

Beverly played the tape of Mr. Jan's speech as I shut my eyes and imagined that I was at the funeral. I took a deep breath and sighed.

"As we mourn the death of my beloved son, Piet Jan, we also mourn the loss of a noble friend and a political activist who believed in what he fought for. I try my best to empathize with the incalculable loss to his girlfriend, whom he loved so dearly. Unfortunately, she could not be with us today, due to her emotional upheaval. The sadness I feel is great. I propose that we, for our own inspiration and consolation, reflect on Piet's life. He was a rare specimen who productively fought to abandon the apartheid system in South Africa. Piet is a symbol of oppression, felt by all those who have no freedom of rights. Piet died because he fell in love with a young woman from the wrong race. He was the paradigm of life, according to virtue. The virtue that I observed in him is the love he shared for all races, cultures, and creeds. He knew no colour barriers. He saw the virtue of humility. He was savagely beaten by those racist police officers, who believe in their hearts that love cannot exist across the colour barrier. The night he was arrested he proposed marriage to his wonderful girlfriend. He had the strength to remain loyal in the face of grave difficulty. With the brutal death of my only son, I will not have the opportunity to have any grandchildren. However, my future grandchildren will be all those children born in South Africa in the next generation: Black, White, Indian, Coloured and any other shades of the *rainbow*. Yes, children born to Mother Africa, in different *shades of the rainbow*. Yes, a *Rainbow Nation*. A *Rainbow Nation*! They will be born into a democratic South Africa. I will see Annelilne (White), Condeleh (Black), Lallitha (brown, Indian) and Jane (Coloured) holding hands and playing together because they know no discrimination. We have to show courage in opening up new doors of knowledge by standing together to abolish this apartheid system in South Africa. We have to cultivate the fields for our freedom. Piet had a vision of our country, where moral virtue of fortitude is essential. Piet's death gives us the incentive to work harder to free all South Africans: Amandla! Amandla! Awetu! Power to the people! Piet's extraordinary, exceptional spirit smiles from above!

"God give me the strength to read out the poem Kay wrote for Piet during their last hours together, as she shared the last amazing hours with him…"

Warm tears streamed down my cheeks, and it sunk in that Piet had passed on.

CHAPTER 11

The Social Class System

I left Durban and headed for the capital city, Pretoria. I thought that the change of environment would help mend my broken heart. Instead of flying I decided to travel by the minivan taxi called a Kombi. This gave me the opportunity to enjoy the scenery as we moved away from the coastal areas. The journey took six hours, and it was amazing.

The most prominent views along the way were of the strong social class system. The Dutch had brought in the apartheid system that separated the races. The British brought in the social class system that separated the upper class, middle class, and lower class within each racial group. Amongst the White racial group, there was only the upper and middle class. Amongst the Indians there was a strong upper class, middle class, and lower class. Most of the Blacks were middle- and lower-class people. Ironically, within the Indian racial group, the different classes did not mix or socialize.

On the way the dilapidated shantytowns of the poor were visible. Their houses were made of corrugated iron sheeting. The shantytowns were compounds of tin shacks, with no electricity or running water. Young children and black women balanced buckets of water on their heads while walking away from the wells. Most of them lived below the poverty line, which was alarming. The enormity of such poverty was inherited from the apartheid era and the settlement of colonial and imperial powers in South Africa.

"I pass this area all the time. These people have no schools, health clinics, malls, water, houses, nothing," said Ahmad the Kombi driver to the passenger sitting next to him.

"No amenities, high levels of structural unemployment—nothing," commented the passenger.

"Oh, you will see a huge gap, the social class gap with all the races as we drive through the residential areas," sighed Ahmad, an Indian Muslim.

"Such inequalities among Blacks—no benefits, no jobs. Our repressive apartheid regime," the passenger continued. He then introduced himself as Saleem, an elementary school teacher from Verulam.

I listened attentively to their conversation about the apartheid regime while observing the impoverished countryside. Most rural dwellers lived on White-owned farms. Others lived in desolate land called African homelands. Little Black children walked around with herds of cattle, directing them with their sjamboks or whips. It was amusing how these Black children yelled at the cows in their Zulu mother tongue, as if that was the language the cow understood. The children stopped to wave at us as we passed. Poverty was due to residential constraints by the enforced evictions of the Apartheid Land Act. The various shantytowns and poor Black settlements along the way overwhelmed me. It was the first time that I had taken a Kombi taxi to Johannesburg. It was as if I were rediscovering the history of South Africa. Coming from an upper-class residential area in Durban, I was not exposed to the elements of poverty that existed in rural areas. This was where the highest rate of sexual assault against women and children occurred. Flying to Johannesburg would not have exposed me to such economic turmoil.

"Those are our gold mines, our precious metals. This is where they extract gold and other minerals from the ground," reported Ahmad as he acted like our tour guide.

"Um, that's capitalism for South Africa," replied Saleem, the passenger.

"Yeah, what a blessing for South Africa, the gold, diamond, and coal mines that bring foreign investors into our country," said Ahmed proudly.

"My uncle worked as an engineer in this gold mine," gloated Saleem. "He worked in the diamond mines in Kimberley too," he continued, revealing his family history.

I felt as if I were revising my history and geography while listening to their conversation. We passed an upper middle-class White neighbourhood with its exclusive, spacious houses. The area had shopping malls, hotels, parks, schools, and ample amenities. The social class differences were so visible. As we stopped at a streetlight, I observed the Black maids crossing the streets with white babies in strollers. Ironically, some of them carried their own black babies tied to their backs while the White babies played with mobiles attached to their strollers. Many Indians and Coloureds walked towards the malls.

As I observed the people crossing, suddenly a Black male in his twenties walked behind an Indian woman and pulled out her thali, a gold necklace worn by married Tamil Indian women as a symbol of marriage. He aggressively yanked it from her neck and ran. People around reacted by holding tightly onto their purses and bags. They were used to such pickpocketing. Ahmed honked several times, but it was no use, the man had disappeared in the crowd. The Indian woman cried as she walked along. Some pedestrians stopped, consoled her, and continued to walk on.

"Did you see that?" exclaimed Ahmad.

"These Indian women in the city deserve that. They enjoy flaunting all their heavy gold jewelry. Look at that one there with an armful of solid, pure gold bangles," said Saleem angrily.

"Yeah, they show off with all their gold jewelry, showing the thieves how rich they are. Those thieves know that," said Ahmad.

The grave concern in the major cities was the high level of criminal activities, like pickpocketing, house break-ins, car hijacking, and other trivial crime. The social class system contributed to the upsurge in crime. It was an unassailable problem brought about by the apartheid era. The White government was apathetic about crime. It did little to combat the problem, which was created by socioeconomic imbalances and racial tension. Violent robberies and murders were on the increase. In the upper-class residential areas, two-meter-high walls with barbed wire on top surrounded huge mansions. The properties looked like prisons. South Africans were prisoners in their own homes because of crimes like house break-ins.

"As the gap between the rich and the poor increases, so does crime. The poor come into the cities to pickpocket innocent people," Ahmad commented.

"Well, crime is a means of survival for the poor. Do you blame them? Poverty breeds criminal activities and high levels of violence," commented Saleem.

A change of ethos was necessary for crime to stop. Saleem and Ahmad engaged in a deep political conversation for about four hours nonstop. At least it was not verbal diarrhea but intellectual conversation, I thought. They were not village idiots but men with high levels of intellectual curiosity. I enjoyed listening to their loud conversation while others in the Kombi just slept. The legacy of crime was evident in that apartheid era. Political repression was continuous and arduous. I believed that some policemen colluded with criminal elements. A lot of crime was committed by juveniles, young Black boys who lived in a society of inequality and poverty. I did not blame them for getting involved in such crime.

"Oh boy, when will this apartheid system end?" sighed Ahmad, slapping his forehead with the palm of his hand.

"Be patient, brother. Allah will mend all problems. Inshalla, inshalla—God's will!" said Saleem in Arabic.

We entered Johannesburg, and it was like entering paradise. The luxurious business and financial district reigned in the heart of the city centre. Its sophisticated buildings, banks, and businesses revealed its materialistic nature. It was such a radical change from the shantytowns of the rural areas. Many white upper-class men walked around in their elegant pin-striped designer suits. The most exquisite glass and chrome buildings surrounded the area, which spelled "wealth." The city was empowered by wealth and luxury. The hotels were trendy, lavish, and elite. It was all created by the municipal boundaries of the apartheid era. It was the commercial centre and residential hub for the rich and famous. The city was busy with the hustle and bustle of people and traffic everywhere.

Lush lawns and well-kept gardens at the centre of the luxurious city gave it a park-like atmosphere. Nowhere in the world could anyone witness such beauty as the contemporary-style buildings nestled in the heart of Johannesburg. It was an indication of the extreme wealth that existed amongst the upper-class Whites, Indians, and Coloureds. The buildings and hotels were built on a grand scale and in a prestigious manner, in proximity to major shopping centres. The city was also home to the consulates of many countries. Johannesburg was vibrant, animated, and alive with the energy of people. Aesthetically appealing condominiums were sandwiched between hotels and commercial buildings. Johannesburg was a vibrant, multicultural city with lots of tourist sights. I could gloat that it was one of the most wealthiest and beautiful cities in the world, with its manicured gardens and charming buildings. Exotic designer stores brightened up the streets. Authentic African crafts were gloriously laid out on the sidewalks.

"I am going to park here at this parking lot. All of you can get out and stretch your legs, visit the toilets, and eat. Yes, have your lunches. Please be back here in exactly an hour so that we can make our way to Pretoria!" yelled Ahmad, as if he were talking to a crowd of people.

"Thank you. I'll see you in an hour," I said and walked away alone.

I went to the bank to withdraw some money for shopping and lunch. There were a lot of juvenile delinquents on the streets begging for money.

"Please, madam, give us some money. I am hungry," begged a little Black boy.

I reached into my pocket and pulled out some loose change. Soon I was surrounded by about eight of them who followed me as if I were a pied piper.

"Madam, madam, please, we want to buy food," they begged obnoxiously. They refused to let me go.

I gave them some more loose change, which they grabbed. Some change fell on the ground, and they began to aggressively fight for it, which gave me a chance to escape.

When I went into the bank to withdraw money, I noticed a beautiful blond White woman in front of me. She looked like a Barbie doll, with soft, long curls. She wore amazing designer jogging pants with a matching bright pink hoodie. She was casually dressed, yet she was from the upper class and looked so elegant.

The bank tellers sat behind a thick bulletproof glass window. There was a small opening on the counter where they slipped me my book and money. Security guards all around scrutinized people entering or leaving. When I had finished, I followed the gracious, elegant blond woman out of the bank. She walked about two metres ahead of me, carrying a Chanel bag.

We walked down the busy sidewalk, and I followed her. Suddenly, a teenage Black youth appeared from behind and pulled down her jogging pants, revealing her leopard-print sexy underwear. Embarrassed, she bent down to pull up her jogging pants while another teenager took her Chanel bag and ran as fast as lightning into the busy crowd.

People were shocked but not surprised. Everyone continued shopping. The nature of altruism was not present. There was no moral obligation to help her. There was no loyalty or a sense of duty to help. No one displayed such ethical thought.

"She should be more careful with her bag, knowing that there are so many thugs around," whispered a passerby to me.

"Yes, careful, but it's horrible!" I exclaimed and walked on.

People did not feel obligated to stop and run after the thugs because they feared for their own lives. The principle of self-sacrifice did not exist. There was no justice for the rich or the poor. I walked past the woman and saw her cry. I pointed to a police vehicle in the distance. She looked and walked towards it. I continued down the luxurious avenues, clutching desperately onto my own bag. I stopped at the designer handbag store and admired the beautiful purses. The arcades with stores were breathtaking with all the high-fashion clothing and accessories. It was a shopping paradise, and shopping was my favourite leisure activity. However, I only had time to window shop.

I reached the end of one luxurious arcade and entered a huge outdoor square, which was just as exotic. Trendy boutiques and the entrance to a glitzy mall surrounded the square. I did not have enough time to explore the stylish shopping mall and the colorful department stores. The square was bustling with exclusive antique markets and stores with exotic collectibles.

The floor of the square featured huge, expensive marble tiles and limestone interlocked with mosaic crystals and swirls of coloured marble in a variety of intriguing patterns. I felt as if I were entering the courtyard of a palace. I spotted numerous restaurants at the far end of the square, which was bustling with people who were well dressed. White and Indian women in their stiletto-heeled shoes walked around elegantly and gracefully. Distinguished businessmen and professionals in suits walked around casually.

I hurriedly entered the square and headed for the restaurant while observing the time on my wristwatch. I exercised caution while walking across the square, still clutching my purse. Suddenly, I felt an intense pain on my exposed right arm. I turned around and looked down. A little Black boy, about ten to twelve years of age, threatened to burn my arm with a lit cigarette. Simultaneously, another little Black boy about the same age tried to rip my handbag away from me, on the left side. I did not care about the lit cigarette because I had too many valuables in my purse. I could not let go of my passport, credit cards, and cash. I fought back, hitting the boy violently with my purse. At the same time, I tried to hit the other one who was trying to burn me. I felt engaged in child abuse. However, I had no other means of defending myself. People were so used to mugging and pickpocketing that they clutched their own handbags and rushed off.

I knew the modus operandi of these children, and I was not going to be a victim of mugging. I knew that I was their target because I'd walked alone. They must have been observing me. As I fought back, hitting and screaming at the top of my voice, an Indian man ran towards me. I recognized him because he'd been in the Kombi. He slapped the boy with the lit cigarette across his face, and the two preteens just laughed and casually walked away.

"I exercised all precautions, yet I was still the target!" I cried.

"Sometimes it is better not to carry a handbag," he replied with a warm smile. "I am Bob, by the way. I noticed you in the taxi from Durban to Johannesburg. I am heading to pick up some quick lunch from the restaurant, so you can join me."

"Thank you, looks like I need protection," I said.

Bob reminded me of my grandfather. He was a helpful, kind, and friendly man in his seventies.

"I just observed a mugging earlier on. I did not imagine that I would be a target," I said, clutching my handbag tightly.

"It's a complicated picture, such a beautiful city and such a high rate of crime," he said.

"The widening gap between the rich and poor. It is relative deprivation that causes these poor children to steal. I felt bad hitting them, but I could not let go of my purse."

"What to do, maa?" he asked with a trace of an old Indian accent and in a fatherly tone.

"Each criminal or pickpocketer on the street has his own modus operandi, method of operation," I added.

I had my eyes peeled as we walked back from the restaurant to the waiting taxi. I became more aware of my surroundings and paid attention to all suspicious behaviour around me. In one day I had witnessed three muggings. I was afraid that I was moving to the crime capital of the world. This was a crime epidemic.

We continued our journey to Pretoria. We dropped a few people off in different luxurious areas. Elaborate mansions stood behind ten-foot-high walls with electric barbed wire on the top. Some houses had private security guards with guns standing at the front gate. Guard dogs were chained onto some gates so that their loud barks would wake up the owners in case of a home invasion or robbery. These were crime prevention strategies among the local Indian community in Pretoria. The barbed-wire walls magnified my anxiety and feelings of insecurity.

For a few days, I lived with friends in their luxurious mansion in an upper-class residential neighbourhood called Laudium. It was a wealthy area. After a week I moved into a flat close by, bordering a lower-class Indian area. South of Laudium were upper-class White residential areas called Erasmia and Christoburg. Just over the green hills from Laudium was an impoverished Black residential area.

To help myself settle down, I got a job as a governess for an affluent Indian family who did not know my background.

Several members of their nuclear and extended family lived in the neighbourhood, within walking distance from each other. Some of them had great pathways and gates to enter each other's mansions. I was the governess for all the children in their family.

Immediately, I noticed the snobbish attitude of the parents, who believed that others were inferior to them. The women were always formally dressed and walked around with a superior attitude. They socialized within their aristocratic social class. They displayed strong bourgeoisie traits. Not all the women were intellectuals, yet they were snobs, due to their personal attributes. They kept their distance from me, and I did not aspire to reveal my background. I continued to move among these social elites as a governess.

The first home I worked at was exquisitely beautiful. It was a three-story mansion, with a west wing and east wing. Each floor had an exotic brass railing around it. From each floor, as one looked down, the enormous indoor pool was visible on the ground floor.

The first day I entered, I did not know what to expect. A butler dressed in uniform opened the door.

"My boss is expecting you, madam," he politely said.

"Thank you," I replied and waved good-bye to the chauffer driving an exotic Mercedes-Benz who'd been sent to pick me up.

The butler led me to an exotic library that filled me with envy and awe. At home I had the ultimate home library, cozy and stocked with books. This massive library was stocked not only with an array of books but also priceless antiques. It was the epic home library that I'd dreamed about. It comprised volumes of books and an amazing art collection. A huge crystal chandelier hung from the steeply vaulted ceiling. The floor was covered in luxurious Persian rugs and the walls with priceless artwork. The dark wood bookcases were elegant, with detailed paneling. The ornate ceilings added class and sophistication. It was such a charming setting. I was a voracious reader, so this was a superb place for me to work, I thought.

As I looked through the windows and admired the impressive gardens, the cook came in.

"Would you like a snack from the kitchen or a drink?" he asked.

He was dressed in a cook's uniform. He was an Indian man from a lower-class background.

"Just water, thank you," I replied.

Just then Mrs. Ali walked in with her children.

"Amazing place. This library is so charming and impressive," I politely complimented her.

"Thank you. You are going to spend a lot of time in this library," she laughed warmly. "And these are my children, Rizwan, age ten, and Mariam, fifteen."

The children were glad to meet me. Once I got to know them well, I realized that they were excited to meet me because their parents were always busy. I became Mariam's teacher, psychologist, confidante, and friend. She loved confiding all her deep, dark secrets in me. According to the Indian Muslim tradition, she was not allowed to date, so she needed someone to confide in. The children did not have the same airs and graces of their parents, and they grew attached to me.

"I have a school talent show and beauty pageant coming up, and you have to come," begged Mariam one day.

"I promise to get you dressed. Is your secret boyfriend going to be there?" I slyly asked.

"Yeah—shush, don't tell anyone," she giggled.

On weekends I did not work. I spent my time alone in my flat. When I was bored and lonely, I looked through the window and observed the Indian people in the adjacent flat. They were so different from the Indians in the mansions. These people were from a lower social class. I shared my flat with another Indian woman and a young White male who'd given up his religion to become a Muslim. Therefore, he only hung out with the Indian Muslim community. His name was Klass. He introduced me to his friends from the next buildings. On one occasion he gave me a ride to the shopping plaza, and I sat in the backseat. He seemed to be so angry that day, which was not like him.

"What's the matter?" I asked. "You do not seem to be yourself."

"Well, other cars with White drivers are giving me strange looks," he replied.

"I do not get why that should be a problem. Is it because you have an Indian girl in the backseat?" I asked with concern.

"No!" he hastily said.

"Articulate!" I abruptly replied.

"Do you not see? You are sitting in the backseat. You make me look like your driver. In South Africa only Black people are drivers for Indians. I am White, I cannot be your driver."

"I am so sorry, Klass. However, if I sit in the front, I will look like your wife, and that is against the Immorality Act. Do you not see that?" I laughed.

"Yes, I see your point of view. I did not think about that," he laughed.

Klass hung out with the Indian group, yet he still had his racial concerns. He introduced me to his friend Fatima, who was Indian. Although Fatima was from a lower social-class background, she immediately welcomed me with open arms. She was a single parent and lived with her teenage daughter,

Fay. They were always so hospitable and often invited me for lunch and dinner with them. Fatima was a great Indian cook. They showed me such respect and always invited me to go shopping with them, which curbed my loneliness. They still displayed polite behaviour and were great at entertaining any stranger. Fatima, her daughter, and their friends were down to earth, and they became my instant friends. They displayed all the ancient ethics of hospitality. Their warm hospitality became a ritual, and they invited me to have dinner with them each day. It was warmth that encompassed me as their family member. I missed the home-cooked meals with my family. The aroma of Fatima's spicy curries and rice when I entered their home made me feel instantly at home.

"Promise us that you will have dinner with us every night?" asked Fatima.

"Hey, you are now part of our family, I reckon," giggled her daughter Fay.

"Thank you. Home is where the heart is. I promise," I replied with a lump in my throat.

"I am taking Fay and her friends to a rock concert next Saturday, will you join us?" Fatima asked kindly.

"Sure, I'd love to," I replied.

Although Fatima came from a lower social class, her hospitality was a gesture of generosity. Most Indians had this nature. It was part of our culture and upbringing, no matter what class we belonged to.

Ironically, I was in a position where I moved daily between families, one from the upper social class and the other from a lower social class. We were all Indians, but I experienced major differences between the classes. The upper class did not mingle with the lower class at any level. In fact, the upper class were unfriendly towards the lower class, which did not bother the lower class. Fatima also became close to me, and she often confided in me.

On one occasion Fatima came to my flat to talk to me.

"I have something important to tell you," she whispered, as if the walls had ears.

"Nothing bad, I hope," I said, showing my interest.

"You are the governess for the Alis' children. Well, do you know that Mr. Ali is having an affair with more than one woman from our flat?" she continued.

"Oh no!" I responded in shock.

"Most of these wealthy Indian men from the surrounding mansions take advantage of single mothers from the lower-class areas," she admitted.

"You've got to be kidding," I gasped, dropping my jaw.

"Mr. Ali sleeps with a few women from around here, Indian women," she said with disgust. "On one occasion he tried to get my daughter Fay to sleep with him. He often looks at her with seductive eyes."

"She's a minor, that is statutory rape. Is he not afraid of contracting AIDS or any other sexual disease? Disgusting." I broadened my eyes as if I saw a ghost. "What a pig!"

"He does not like me because I would not give in to his sexual needs. I may be poor, but I am not cheap. My dignity is intact. Most of these women want their money," she said.

"Does his wife know?" I asked.

"I don't know. Maybe the women don't care. Money brings such corruption," she replied.

"Tell me about it," I added sarcastically.

Mariam's talent show and beauty pageant arrived. I spent hours with her, helping her polish herself. Mrs. Ali was young, in her thirties, and she went out of her way to look just as beautiful on that day. Before we left for Mariam's school, I was invited to have dinner with the family. It was the first time that I'd met Mr. Ali. He displayed such a snobbish, aristocratic attitude as he sat at the head of the luxurious dinner table like a king in his castle. In my mind I replayed what Fatima had told me, and I thought that he made an excellent actor, playing the role of the perfect father and husband. He was in his late thirties or early forties, and his wealth had been passed onto him through generations. I displayed the same etiquette as the family, with the conversational skills and social behaviour of the upper class, which seemed to shock him.

Dinner was formal and we were allocated seats. The utensils and cutlery were formal as well. We engaged in conversation with those to the right or left of us, not across the table as we did at Fatima's dinners, which were informal. The cook brought in garnished grilled lamb served with a medley of fresh, colourful vegetables. The second course was chicken curry served with saffron rice. The butler walked around and topped each adult's glass with wine and poured juice for the children. It was a feast with the social elite. I was surprised that wine was served at a Muslim home.

The talent show was held at a prestigious private school, attended by children from the upper social class. That private school had a weird twist. The children were not all Indians. They also belonged to the upper-class White, Indian, Coloured, and Black groups. They all socialized as one.

"That is the daughter of the French ambassador," said Mrs. Ali as she pointed out a girl singing in the school band.

"That's amazing!" I replied.

"Most of the White children you see here belong to ambassadors from different countries," she gloated.

"Really!" I exclaimed.

"And that is the great-granddaughter of Nelson Mandela," she continued to boast.

"I'm impressed, he is such a hero!" I acknowledged.

"Do you think my hair looks good tonight?" she asked with blatant vanity.

"It's beautiful," I assured her.

"Why, thank you," she replied with a British accent, which was common to all South African Indians of the upper class.

At the concert Mrs. Ali seemed more relaxed and developed a friendlier attitude towards me.

"Mariam adores you," she said tenderly.

"You've raised a wonderful daughter," I praised her.

"I wish you could be with us forever. I want you to be there when she gets married too," she said passionately.

"Only time will tell," I replied.

The students showcased their unique talents in acting, singing, playing instruments, classical dancing, tribal dancing, modern dance, acrobatics, and reciting poetry. Mrs. Ali was nervous when Mariam was onstage because students were to receive first, second, and third place awards. The students displayed such zaniness and commitment in their acts of grandeur, which were spectacular and surprising.

Mariam was captivating with her classical dancing. She had a special dance instructor who'd helped her practice. She'd rehearsed daily for hours to arrive at perfection.

"I am going to chat with one of the judges," said Mr. Ali. "She is the wife of my close friend."

"Put in a good word for Mariam," said Mrs. Ali.

"Oh yes, I will," he replied.

"Invite her and her family for dinner," said Mrs. Ali.

"For sure, I will," he sarcastically giggled.

I listened to them and wondered if they were trying to bribe their way through this talent show. I thought it a lack of integrity. When it came to honesty, I rode the moral horse.

Then I thought about Mr. Ali cheating on his wife with women from the lower social class, and I realized that his infidelity was also dishonesty. Dishonesty to him was like a roller coaster ride with all its joy and excitement.

"He drives me crazy, sometimes he is so verbally abusive," Mrs. Ali said. I was surprised that she confided in me. "I wish I was alone, without him."

"Well, you might as well be alone than be with someone and wish that you were alone," I advised her.

"Well said," she replied.

"He enjoys going to swinging clubs, which upsets me," she confided.

"Swingers' clubs!" I exclaimed. "Wife swapping?"

"He's crazy. Just keep it to yourself. Do not mention this to anyone, promise?" she pleaded.

"Scouts honour," I agreed.

I was surprised that Mrs. Ali had reached her comfort zone and was prepared to confide in me. That night I saw a more subtle side of her. She acknowledged me as a friend, not just a governess to her children. I saw a lonely person who needed someone to talk to.

"I cannot mention this to my sisters-in-law. They can be so cattish," she whispered. "There is so much jealousy and clash of personalities amongst us."

"Family politics occurs in all families, not just your family," I consoled her.

The whole idea of swinging and swingers disgusted me. However, I had to listen to and advise her. Inside I felt so guilty because I was harbouring a great secret, what Fatima had told me. I'd promised Fatima that I would keep it a secret. My mouth was sealed, and I was not the type to reveal any secrets. I had to have an inner dialogue with myself, to promise myself "mum's the word." I took a vow of silence.

"Promise not to mention what I told you," Mrs. Ali begged.

"Trust me, I promise," I assured her.

"Thank you. What would I do without you?"

The judges went onstage to announce the winners. Mr. and Mrs. Ali were so nervous. They were used to giving their children everything. However, this was out of their control. The judges announced the third place winner, which was Mariam. I applauded with excitement. Mr and Mrs. Ali seemed upset.

"Lighten up, at least she is in the top three," I said.

"Yes, we are grateful, happy," nodded Mrs. Ali.

"My daughter is the best," said Mr. Ali.

"I agree," I replied.

After the talent show, we drove home. When the chauffer navigated the Mercedes into the driveway, Mr. Ali told his wife that he would give me a ride to my flat because the chauffer wanted to return home to his family. I immediately smelled a rat.

I calmly agreed, and on the way home Mr. Ali's snobbish attitude changed.

"Where are you from?" he asked in a polite tone.

"Durban," I replied.

"What's your family's surname?"

"You would not know them," I evaded the subject.

"You seem so polished, so upper social class."

"Really!" I did not want to reveal my background to him.

I then believed what Fatima had told me about him. He was a womanizer. He knew the art of seduction. I was appalled by his behaviour.

"You are so beautiful," he complimented.

"So is your wife," I sarcastically replied.

"You have a boyfriend?"

"Yes, I do," I lied.

"You have a beautiful figure," he flirted.

"So do your wife and daughter," I sarcastically remarked.

Images of Piet sped through my mind, and I wanted to burst out crying. Then Mr. Ali's hands touched mine, and he gently stroked my fingers. This happened in front of my flat, as I was about to exit the car. I pulled my hands away. He leaned forward to kiss me, and I pushed his face away.

"Stop! I am not that type!" I yelled "Even if they cremated me with you, I would not feel the heat. You are disgusting!" I yelled.

I got out of the car as soon as it stopped and hastily ran up the stairs to my flat on the second floor. I jumped into bed and sobbed hysterically. I realized that I could no longer live in Pretoria and deal with such a superficial life. The social class system was too evident and inhumane. The apartheid error was an *error of era*.

CHAPTER 12

It's Sad to Say Good-Bye

I did not think the day would arrive that I'd have to leave South Africa. The political laws were getting more lenient, but the hope for complete change was yet to come. The sadness of losing those close to me was hard to bear. I'd tried moving to another city, but I'd faced the same racial segregation. The social class system inherent in the apartheid rule caused havoc in the cities. It is hard to say good-bye to the country of one's birth, but sometimes it is necessary.

I immigrated to Canada, a country that takes care of its new-comers in humanitarian tradition. What fascinated me most was the multicultural atmosphere. The main ideology was to provide freedom for all people. I settled in the major city of Toronto and lived in a diverse and multicultural society. I rented a small bachelor apartment and enjoyed moving around in such a safe environment. Ethnicity was celebrated, people living together in peace and harmony side by side. I blended into a vibrant cultural mosaic where each group displayed mutual respect for the others. It was such a fascinating experience. Toronto was also a magnet for other immigrants, which made me feel comfortable. English was my mother tongue and first language, so that made life easier. The city was peaceful and safe, the people welcoming and friendly. Toronto had a reputation for attracting people from various parts of the globe who then made it their permanent home. I was happy that I'd propelled myself in that direction because I arrived in a city I had envisioned all my life. It was not difficult getting a job, as there was equal opportunity for all.

What I had to get used to was living alone after coming from an extended family unit. There were moments of terror and nightmares. I rarely had company, not knowing many people in the city. There were days when I whimpered and made a lot of collect calls to South Africa. When I was at work, I was happy to be surrounded by people. To help combat the paranoia associated with loneliness, I took on several jobs, which helped in my socialization process.

I was not going to live a life of solitude, so at night I got a second job as a babysitter for a European couple who worked night shifts. They had three daughters, aged four, six, and ten, who were adorable, and they kept me entertained at night. I took the babysitting job because it helped me combat loneliness. The girls' mother, Lisa, had advertised at a local library that she was looking for a babysitter. The first day I met her, I was fascinated by her questions.

"Hi, I'm Lisa, nice to meet you," she introduced herself in a friendly manner. "Where do you come from?"

"I'm from South Africa," I replied.

"But you look Paki!" she said.

"I have not heard that term before," I said, looking at her curiously.

I later found out that "Paki" was slang for people from Pakistan, or even those of Indian descent. I was amused by the term.

"What does a South African look like?" I laughed.

"I don't know, never met one. I thought that they were all black," she naively replied.

"There are millions of Indians in South Africa," I advised her.

"Hey, Dave, come meet our new babysitter. She is South African!" she yelled to her husband.

He hurriedly came into the living room. He was just as friendly as his wife and welcomed me into their home with such hospitality. They were a young couple in their thirties, of Romanian decent.

"I have friends from South Africa too," he said excitedly.

"Which part of South Africa?" I inquired.

"They are from Somalia," he replied.

"That's a totally different country," I laughed. "Africa is a continent. South Africa and Somalia are two totally different countries on the continent of Africa. It is like comparing Italy to Portugal. They are two different countries in Europe." It was as if I were giving him a lesson in geography.

We all laughed and he summoned his three daughters.

"Hey, this is your new friend and babysitter from South Africa. She is so beautiful," chorused both parents.

"Do you live with lions, tigers, and elephants in South Africa?" asked the ten year old.

"Yes, and they eat little children," I laughed.

"You live in a jungle? Do you know Tarzan?" asked the six year old. "You jump from tree to tree too?" she curiously asked.

"Yes, and our Santa, whom we call Father Christmas, comes swinging from tree to tree. Sometimes he comes on a surfboard too," I joked. "I will show you pictures of South Africa. It is a beautiful country with summer-like weather all year round," I warmly smiled.

The parents were just as naïve as the children as they asked about the history and geography of South Africa. I took the job not for the money but for the company, and my plan worked well. I bonded with the mother, father, and children. They enjoyed my company. I often told them my stories from South Africa, and they listened attentively. Conveying events of my past through words and narrating cultural stories was like psychological therapy for me. It helped me recall memories of my past, which made me happy. It helped me maintain my cultural values while integrating into a new Western culture. I felt committed to the memories of my South African lifestyle. Through me the family, especially the children, also learned more about my culture. The parents told me stories of their past, which were just as interesting. Storytelling was the way of bridging the gap between cultures. I realized that my life was constructed into a coherent plot line.

A year passed and I became closer to the family. One Friday night the parents returned home at two in the morning. I did not ask them but wondered what job would finish at two in the morning. I knew Lisa was a psychic. They did mention that they hung out at the racetracks a lot, but I did not delve deeper into their personal or business life.

"We are so sorry about being late. We were caught up with business," said Dave.

"The children are asleep. I will catch a cab home," I whispered.

I called a taxi and waited outdoors in the cold for the taxi to arrive. The temperature was below freezing, and it was beginning to snow.

"Hey, there!" I heard a voice and swiftly turned around. It was Dave.

"I think that I'm falling in love with you," he whispered.

"What are you talking about?" I said, stunned.

I was in shock and disbelief because I hadn't suspected anything. I looked over my right shoulder and spotted Lisa at the end of the passage. She was observing us.

The next day at work, I repeated the story to a girlfriend that I had become close to.

"Oh my God. You need to quit. What if he comes home late at night while his wife is at work and rapes you?" Mandy sounded concerned.

"That's food for thought. Yes, you may be right," I replied.

"Call them and tell them that you cannot babysit because you have extra hours at work. Do you want me to call them for you?" she asked.

"Yes, that will avoid further questioning," I replied with a scared tone.

Mandy had my back. She was a white Canadian with beautiful blue eyes and blond hair. Most of all she had a heart of gold.

To help my loneliness at home and meet more friends in my new country, I decided to do a lot of volunteering at different charitable organizations. I also felt the urgent psychological need to help and give back to others, since I had had such a lucky and fortunate life. Volunteering also enabled me to improve my quality of life and gain experience. I also felt the need to share my skills with others. I was a selfless person who believed in helping others without getting paid. I felt a sense of moral goodness when I helped others.

I had several interesting volunteer jobs, which I enjoyed tremendously and which gave me the opportunity to meet lots of friends from different cultures. I most enjoyed working at a nonprofit organization that helped new immigrants from all over the globe. I ran many interesting programs for newcomers who did not speak English. I did my best to help them by providing support and intervening in times of crisis. My educational background and postgraduate studies in counselling made me a suitable candidate to counsel these refugees, who were affiliated with international organizations. I enjoyed every moment as a volunteer, helping those who were so vulnerable.

After volunteering with the immigrants for a year, I was called up by the senior coordinator.

"Everyone here is so impressed by your hard work, we do not want to lose you," he said.

"I'm here to stay and help you from the bottom of my heart," I sincerely replied.

The senior coordinator was a black African man named Mac, originally from Somalia. He was a friendly and genuine person.

I made friends with other volunteers who taught English as well. Lorry was an Italian girl who was really friendly. I spent a lot of time chatting with her during our breaks. Catherine was a hippie-looking Canadian white woman of Irish background whom I also became friendly with. We helped with an array of services, such as befriending immigrants, organizing social events, and teaching English as a second language. Once when Catherine, Lorry, and I were together, Lorry pointed something out.

"There are paid positions for ESL teachers," she said.

"Are any available? How do you apply?" asked Catherine.

"Well, the volunteers who teach ESL have first choice in getting a position when it becomes available. We have to have patience," replied Lorry.

"As it stands, I am in first position to take the next available ESL teacher's position, followed by you, Lorry, and then Kay," Catherine explained.

Each Sunday I sat on the cold step waiting for Catherine to open the doors. She was religiously late, which annoyed me. I reminded myself that I was there to serve the diversity of clients and to relate to them interpersonally. I genuinely enjoyed interacting with new immigrants. It was not long before Catherine got a paid position as a permanent teacher of English as a second language. That meant that I worked under her. She was so busy delegating jobs that she had no time to socialize.

In a matter of months, another ESL teacher quit and Lorry took over her job. Soon it had gone to her head. All the ESL volunteers worked under her, and her attitude changed. She was not as friendly as she used to be. She became grouchy and wanted work done her way. She was always in a bad mood with magnified crankiness.

On one particular day, my bus was stuck in traffic. I was about ten minutes late, and my class patiently waited for me.

"Where have you been? You are late!" Lorry obnoxiously yelled.

"I was stuck in traffic," I explained.

"That's no excuse! You should leave home early!" she continued to aggressively yell.

"I am just a volunteer," I announced.

She had nothing more to say and ushered me into the classroom. I could not believe her demeaning ways. When she and Catherine were volunteers, they were always late. I was the one waiting patiently for them outside in the cold. She was trying to imitate someone with power. The ambiguity of the situation was that she was also late at times. She was dealing with immigrant refugees who'd escaped from nasty political situations, yet she behaved and mimicked such authoritative behaviour. Lorry created a toxic environment.

Soon my turn came around. Catherine had moved to another province, and I was next in line to take over her paid position. I was so excited because I had been with the organization for over a year. Their policy had always been when one paid teacher leaves, the next volunteer in line fills the position.

"Hi, Lorry, may I talk to you about the available ESL position?" I politely asked.

"Well, I got together with the board of directors, and we decided to conduct interviews of those who apply for the position," she uttered.

"OK, well, I'll apply then," I politely said.

After the interview I was convinced that I would get the job. But I was informed by Lorry that the position was given to another person who was not even involved at the centre. I felt as if I'd been treated with disrespect and contempt. When I eventually met the new ESL teacher, everything fell into place as I analyzed the situation. She was a hippie-looking woman, with blond hair and eyelashes. I hadn't acknowledged the obvious: all the English as a second language teachers were predominantly white. I was the ethnic minority. This seemed like workplace racial discrimination. There was a lack of appropriate accommodations for racial and ethnic minorities. I confronted Lorry with the problem.

"What went wrong at the interview?" I asked. "I had all the experience and was next in line to fulfill the position."

"Well, the new teacher answered one question better than you did," she said, giving a lame excuse.

"And the question was...?" I asked.

"If you were a bank teller, how would you handle an immigrant who did not speak English? You answered the question incorrectly. The new teacher answered it correctly," she answered, giving another lame excuse.

"But I am not a bank teller," I said, shaking my head in disgust. "Did she get the position because she is white?"

The blood rushed to Lorry's head and her face turned fifty shades of red. This was my first encounter with racism in the host country, although it was not stated in law, as in South Africa. When the law itself was racist, it was easier to accept than when discrimination was done in such a cunning manner. Lorry was in charge of the decision-making process, and it was apparent that she'd implemented her own racial biases when choosing the candidate. As a member of an ethnic minority group, this racially oppressive environment narrowed my viable career options. I went home and vowed never to go back. I could not believe that racism was so ripe in this host country in terms of employment. Ironically, the clients the centre served were from minority groups as well. Canada was a tossed salad, a place where all races lived together yet maintained their cultural ties. The United States of America was a melting pot where all immigrants blended, but as Americans.

I got a call from Mr. Mac.

"We have not seen you in two weeks, and you did not even call," he said. He sounded so genuine. "You are our best volunteer, and we do not want to lose you."

I explained the situation to him and told him how disgusted I was to experience such discrimination, prejudice, and social isolation. He was very upset and claimed that he would get Lorry to apologize to me.

"I am sorry about what happened and how you feel," said Lorry the next day on the phone. "We would like you to share the job with the other teacher, where you would get paid every alternate week," she nervously uttered.

"Racist attitudes, assumptions, stereotypes, discrimination, and institutional racism are not what I expected from the centre. No, thank you," I said and abruptly ended the call.

After leaving South Africa, I was committed to equality for all. I was in search of positive experiences in my host country. I was not going to hit the ceiling of racial discrimination in my career prospects. I needed to progress further in my career path. I believed that Lorry was classically conditioned to see minorities only as clients, not as figures of power or position. I quit my volunteer position, because I did not receive the respect I deserved.

CHAPTER 13

Home Away from Home

I felt homesick away from my native country. Instead of allowing myself to feel depressed or bewildered, I integrated myself fully into my new lifestyle by joining a lot of other volunteer organizations, in the mental health field. This helped combat my homesickness. I did not allow myself to be alone or isolated. Volunteering helped me meet new friends and I enjoyed a diversity of new experiences. Meeting others made me realize that others had similar experiences. I missed the hot sun, my favourite foods, and the ambience of the places I used to hang out with friends.

Seeing people of different cultures was part of my cultural shock. Establishing new friendships gave me the sense of belonging. On one particular occasion, I met my friend Mandy for lunch and she asked me to accompany her to a local flea market. We took the bus there, which felt so safe. I was not accustomed to traveling by bus. The whole experience was so pleasant. As the bus moved along, Mandy was like a tour guide, introducing me to new places along the way. Through her I learned to live in a diverse society.

"You've been here for almost two years. Have you adjusted to Canadian living?" asked Mandy.

"Oh yes, I have, especially when I am with friends like you. I do feel homesick when I am alone," I replied.

"The way you work, you are never alone. I think you just use your apartment to sleep in," chuckled Mandy.

"I agree. However, I need to embrace the Canadian accent," I laughed.

"You speak English with a sort of British accent, which is so adorable," said Mandy.

"Old dogs can't learn new tricks. I will not lose my South African English accent," I giggled.

"Your advantage is that you speak English, so it makes integration into our Canadian society easier," commented Mandy.

"However, Canadian pronunciation of words is not the same as the English that I speak," I sighed.

"Canadians roll the R too much, whereas the English R is hardly pronounced," Mandy lectured.

"Yes. *Car*, *bar*, shark," I added.

"Ve are the Vipers, ve vish to vash and vipe your vindows!" she retorted some German accent she had read in a book.

"Vy, wery vell done!" I imitated her as we clowned around.

On our way we analyzed accents, which made for an interesting conversation. When we arrived at the flea market, it was so pleasant getting items at a discount price. Mandy and I had fun purchasing items that we could not find at the mall.

While choosing movies on DVD, my ears were drawn to the young couple next to me. Immediately, I felt as if I'd been transported back to South Africa. I listened to them with amazement because they had strong South African accents. It was so fascinating listening to the accent again. I looked up at them and smiled, and they smiled back.

"Are you South Africans?" I asked.

"Yes!" they replied in chorus.

"Recognized the accent," I smiled.

"All those years and we did not lose it," chuckled the male.

"Which part of South Africa do you come from?" I asked.

"Durban," said the female.

"Bingo—that's where I came from too!" I exclaimed.

They later introduced themselves as Mano and Chris. They were both from Durban and of Indian descent. They were brother and sister, and their parents were lawyers. Chris and his father had both been locked up as political prisoners because of their active involvement with the African National Congress.

We walked to the food court. Mandy and I were so interested to hear of Chris's experience.

"I was a university student long before you. Unrest on campus was rife because of the political tension in the country. My dad and I became members of the African National Congress to fight for the dismantling of the apartheid system," he went on.

Chris told us about his horrific experiences in prison as we attentively listened. He explained how he was tortured, to extract confessions from him. He and his father had just returned from an underground ANC meeting when they felt that they were being followed. They tried entering the highway and then side roads in order to lose the car following them. Eventually, after an hour of pursuit, they were bumped from the back and had to pull over. Two undercover police officers arrested them and took them into solitary confinement.

"Oh my God, they must have been observing you and your father's activities for a while," I said, shocked.

"Yes!" he replied. "Watching, stalking, observing."

They were not allowed to express their views during the apartheid era, Chris explained. They were taken into solitary confinement at a secret detention centre. They found themselves with other detainees who were journalists, university students, doctors, lawyers, and intellectuals. Special integration officers violated the international human rights law when they chained the detainees and severely beat them.

"They wanted to silence us by the systematic use of solitary confinement and physical torture," Chris said, tears filling his eyes.

"Your father was always with you?" I asked.

"No, he was transported to Robben Island off Cape Town, and we did not hear from him."

Chris was placed in a hostile environment where he was hung upside down from the ceiling and severely beaten, he told us. Several political activists and journalists found themselves in the same situation. They were locked up individually in small cells with just a mat of dried grass on the floor. Chris's room was cold, and he was stripped down to his underwear. At night he could feel the cold concrete floor through the mat. There was no ventilation, and he felt claustrophobic. He had a panic attack, knowing that he could not escape. He felt as if he was being suffocated. He was confined to the cell for weeks.

"I understand how you must have felt. I do empathize with you because I had a similar experience, going against the Immorality Act," I said, as I felt that pain again.

"Really," said Mano, "you too?"

Chris told us that after a few days, he was taken out of his cell. He'd been given no food or water that day and had felt very weak. A guard opened the cell and passed him a bowl of sour porridge for breakfast. It was made of grainy corn flour, water, and salt. Although it tasted bad, Chris ate it with pleasure to combat his hunger. After breakfast Chris asked the guard if he could use the toilet, and the guard yelled.

"What, man? You think this is your luxury home? Hou stil, man." (Be quiet, man.)

The guard spoke a combination of English and Afrikaans. He handed Chris a small, old-fashioned metal bucket to use as a toilet. Chris perceived the situation as imminent danger, because throughout that night he had to smell the stench of feces from the bucket, which made him vomit. He was then faced with the smell of vomit in his small cell, and his anxiety level rose.

"God forbid. That's so inhumane!" cried Mandy.

"That's the apartheid era," I added.

"All political prisoners were given the same treatment," explained Chris.

Chris felt an irrational fear, he told us. To keep his sanity, he counted all the little black bugs and cockroaches that walked in a row along the room's skirting boards. They looked like an army, walking to the tone of the sergeant's command. He counted each one. He even allowed them to crawl over his fingers and onto the palms of his hands. They became his close network of friends.

For lunch he was given a bowl of samp, a combination of various beans and corn flour cooked in thick stew.

"I missed Mom's curried chicken and biryani. I was a picky eater at home and complained if the curry or biryani was too spicy," he laughed.

"You had no choice. I am sure you then appreciated your mom's cooking," added Mandy.

Chris was not allowed to communicate with the other prisoners. Isolation was a traumatic and horrendous experience.

"My dad, on the other hand, was subjected to hard labor on Robben Island. He had to clean up his own bucket of feces. He shivered when he cleaned up his own stools, studying their shape, size, texture, weight, and smell just to keep his mind occupied," said Mano.

"What's Robben Island?" asked Mandy.

Chris explained that it was an island in Table Bay, off the coast of Cape Town. "It was a small island, about three kilometres long and two kilometres wide, that housed all political prisoners in South Africa, including Nelson Mandela and Jacob Zuma. Those who tried to escape drowned. All political prisoners faced brutal tyranny and oppression during the apartheid regime. All political prisoners were exiled there, and it became a maximum security prison."

He swallowed a lump in his throat. Tears streamed down his flustered cheeks. "My dad had no contact with the outside world!" he cried.

"He was in isolation and my mom was going crazy," said Mano.

"Oh my God!" said Mandy in shock.

"That's the meagerness of prison life," explained Chris.

"That is why we appreciate this host country and its democracy," I proudly added.

Chris explained how he and Mano felt the pain of leaving South Africa but immigrated to Canada for a safe political life. Their mother, who is a lawyer, stayed behind in case she could get a chance to visit with their father. Chris and Mano also fell in love with the host country and its democratic feel, they told us, but missed the atmosphere of South Africa with its hot, tropical climate. In Canada, Chris and Mano could continue their postgraduate studies peacefully.

I kept in touch with these new friends. On one cold winter day, February 2, 1990, I received a call from Mano.

"Did you hear the news? State President F. W. de Klerk took away the ban on the African National Congress and other antiapartheid organizations. He is going to release all political prisoners!" she excitedly cheered.

"Seize the moment! That is the end of this era of error, the apartheid regime in South Africa. I cannot believe this amazing news!" I said and jumped for joy.

"You reckon so? Peace and reconciliation!" she cried.

I hugged my pillow and looked up to the ceiling, thanking God for the good news. I jumped on my bed, laughed, cried, and yelled to my heart's content.

I got together with Chris and Mano, and we all cuddled up in front of the television as if we were watching a hockey game. Our eyes were glued to the television. We silenced all other sounds in the room and raised the volume of the television.

Tears of joy streamed down our faces as Mr. Nelson Mandela approached the gates of Victor Verster Prison in Paarl with his wife. They walked hand in hand, a journey of freedom. He looked so handsome and elegant in his brown suit and matching tie. Chris, Mano, and I animatedly threw our fists in the air, giving a victory salute. We felt that ecstatic moment with such passion. Mandela got into a silver luxury BMW and headed for Cape Town.

I cried because I could not be there at that special rally. I'd been at all the other rallies held in South Africa and felt the crowd's passion. But I still felt the emotion as I watched people dance in the streets on TV. Peopled clamored to see their hero and to celebrate the end of years of oppression and oppressive government.

"Piet is watching from above!" I cried. "How proud he would have been to witness this special moment in South Africa's history!"

I sobbed like a baby, and Mano gave me a hug of consolation.

"I understand, it must be hard," she said. "He passed away fighting to abolish the apartheid system and its Immorality Act."

We listened attentively as the politicians gathered on the balcony of the city hall in Cape Town. Tons of people assembled to hear Nelson Mandela's words of wisdom:

> Our struggle has reached a decisive moment. Our march to freedom is irreversible. Now is the time to inten-sify the struggle on all fronts. To relax now would be a mistake which future generations would not forgive. Today the majority of South Africans, black and white, recognize that apartheid has no future. It has ended by our own decisive mass action in order to build peace and security. The mass campaign of defiance and other actions of our organization and people can only culmi-nate in the establishment of democracy. The destruction caused by apartheid on our subcontinent is incalculable.

Mandela's powerful words echoed through the crowd. I felt intense joy and my world was suddenly filled with hap-piness that transcended the room. Suffering, disappointments, and failure had come to an abrupt end, and my life became self-fulfilled. The days of resentment, depression, hopelessness, hatred, anger, and torment vanished into thin air. Our minds had been programmed since early childhood to accept a law that treated people—men, women, and children—unfairly. The congested feeling in my head was erased. A positive energy flowed through my body.

I looked about the room and noticed that each one's eyes were filled with tears. It was a bittersweet moment. The oxymoron was realized by all of us in the room: We felt the sweet joy of witnessing the end of the apartheid era. Conversely, we felt the bitterness of not being in South Africa to witness such a historic moment. After all, we'd attended every rally to abolish the apartheid system.

"Thank God for television—we are able to witness such an iconic moment!" cried Mano.

"I would have loved to have attended," I sobbed.

That night at home, I could not sleep. My mind raced as I thought about the country of my birth. All my experiences— social, political, psychological, and emotional—flashed before me. My heart pounded with joy and sadness. The television news channels and documentaries had featured repeated information about the end of the apartheid era and I'd watched each one attentively.

It was past midnight, and I still could not sleep. I was in a state of shock, trying to digest all the information I'd seen. I took out my diary to record all that had happened on that auspicious day. It was the best way to vent all my feelings and hidden emotions.

> Dear Diary,
> It is the end of the apartheid era,
> A period of torture and even terror.
> South Africa, the country of my birth,

Where God placed me upon his earth.
It was a system that was so wrong,
My experiences made me so strong.
Blacks, Coloureds, Indians, and Whites,
Non-Whites were given absolutely no rights.
Demonstrations could no longer be passive,
Restrictions were unrealistic and massive.
South Africa needed international mediation
To get rid of the laws of such deviation.
Mr. de Klerk held a long media debate
To address the critical issue of racial hate.
White South Africans with the best resources,
Violent racial action from the police forces,
Non-Whites were not allowed to vote.
Dear Diary, this is an important note,
For years we faced racial segregation
That led to vicious human degradation.
When non-Whites cast their first vote,
A time for all South Africans to gloat.
Proud to live in a country that's free,
I am so excited and happy as can be.
My mood can be described as buoyant,
The apartheid system was so flamboyant.
South Africa will not experience oppression,
Its people free of such depression,
We would all be loyal to democracy,
The end of all South African autocracy.
Black, red, green, blue, white, and gold,
Colours of the new South Africa flag are bold.
South Africans sing "Nkosi Sikelel' iAfrika"
To celebrate the end of colour bar.
The lyrics of the old anthem people despised,

Words of the new anthem were revised.
All the precious stones below the soil,
The apartheid system we needed to recoil.
Dear Diary! For men and woman who risked lives,
Freedom for all South Africans now thrives.
Dear Diary! I shed tears of joy,
For each South African girl or boy
Of every culture and every race,
A democratic South Africa they face.
Holding hands to form a rainbow,
All colors of a nation in a row,
They will learn to live in peace.
Dear Diary! I hope for violence to decrease,
I dream of the present and erase the past,
I did not think that apartheid would last.
Dear Diary! Those happy, cheering faces
Acknowledging all the different races,
The end of the system of repression,
The end of a system of severe depression.
Dignitaries and world leaders celebrate
June 3, 1993, as such a historic date.
Dear Diary! As I stare at my television,
South Africans celebrate a new vision.
It evokes all my senses, especially of sight,
South Africans celebrate a democratic plight,
Freedom regardless of the color of the skin.
Dear Diary! I celebrate this glorious win
With a sense of renewed hope.
In the future will they finally cope?
I think about the heartbreak of my past,
The interracial relationship did not last.
Dear Diary! I cannot help but cry,

To change my mood I'll gracefully try.
I lived through the apartheid era,
A system that was an era of error.
Thank you, dear Diary, for sharing my tale,
Celebrating the release of those from jail.
Thank you, dear Diary, for helping me cope
And go on living with intense hope.

At last, I closed my eyes and fell asleep. My diary was my best friend, the one whom I always confided in. Putting words to paper was a form of psychological therapy, allowing me to vent all my emotions and feeling. I slept peacefully knowing that the nightmare of my past had ended.

It must have been way past midnight when I heard a click at the front door of my bachelor apartment. It was a strange click, as if someone had turned the doorknob. The room was dark. I did not know what danger lurked behind such darkness. I was all alone and wondered what the darkness concealed. I felt a degree of fear. I did not suffer from achluophobia; I was used to being alone in the dark. Suddenly, I heard footsteps. Someone dragged his or her feet across the carpeted floor. My subconscious mind triggered a sense of fear. I covered my head with a blanket and froze. The fluff of the blanket tickled the tip of my nose, and I tried to suppress my sneeze.

I peered from under my blanket into the darkness beyond as silence fell. Time stood still. The footsteps crept closer. I trembled with fear as the muscles of my toes involuntarily twitched. I listened intently. I kept my breathing low. The footsteps paused for a short duration. I felt as if I were in a séance. I felt an energetic breeze around me, then an eerie feeling came over me. The chill in the room was exaggerated. I shut my eyes tight and held my breath. My hand moved involuntary. I did not know who'd entered my room. The footsteps came to a halt at my bed. I felt a sudden breeze over me; the room became drafty. It felt as if a supernatural predator was in my room. I wondered if there was going to be a struggle. It got to my nerves, and I felt chilly. A soft, droopy hand touched my covered body. I felt a limp feeling and thought that I was going to be strangled. I waited patiently for the gruesome hands of my killer to strangle me. I did not move. Neither did I break the silence. A limp body moved over mine. I was not prepared for self-defense. He did not place his entire weight over me. I felt as if I were in a state of dystopia.

To my right the bed sank, as if someone had plopped next to me. I felt the mattress compress. I felt the person's presence. My heart began to race. I could not breathe. I felt goose bumps on my thighs. I felt cold spots around me. I felt a strong and distinct denseness of energy on the bed, right next to me. I knew a human body lay next to me. My body was alerted to some paranormal activity, which challenged my intelligence and awareness.

I felt an extrasensory perception. I could not move. Whomever it was stroked my cheek, and I lost my breath. My voice went on strike. It refused to come out. I had a tingling feeling all over my body. I felt as if someone were observing me in sleep. The hand touched my neck and I froze. I was in a catatonic state; I could not move or speak. It was surreal. I felt fully aware rather than asleep. As the person softly pressed the bed around me, I waited patiently for the next move. I felt a wave of current run through my body. It did not hurt, so I did not react. My energy was drained. The hand that stroked my neck was rough. It felt enormous. I felt the dry, chapped skin stroke my soft skin. I did not know if it was the manifestation of a spirit.

Suddenly, a mysterious fragrance wafted out of nowhere, a telltale sign. It was the heavenly scent of Piet, my deceased boyfriend, the perfume he used to wear. I immediately felt comforted by this paranormal phenomenon. It brought painful emotions. I was still raw from grieving over him. I sensed that he was whole and healthy, with no sense of pain. I wondered if it was a momentary visit.

I was lucid and felt as if I could manipulate the situation. The whole experience was so realistic and vivid. I was the silent observer trying to capture each inspirational moment while maintaining self-control. I was keenly aware of Piet's contemplation and presence. I felt an overwhelming desire to keep every moment alive. The room was dark, and his presence was strong.

It was so moving for me that I began to sob hysterically. Piet embraced me as I sobbed. It was the first time a spirit had visited me. I felt a yearning, like I wanted the moment to last forever. I surrendered completely to his touch. Although I was so frightened by his appearance, I responded as if he were there in the flesh. He offered me comfort in that time of grief. It was a moment I hadn't prepared for and my deepest pain and fear were manifest. I felt my astral body leave my physical body.

I was in a state of astral catalepsy. I felt as if I were astrally traveling, which was a strange phenomenon. I seemed to be in a state of motion while my physical body slept. I was pulled from my horizontal position, and I appeared to be vertical. That was a special moment. Piet gave me a spiritual clarity, and I gained a deeper understanding of the circumstances that had separated Piet and me. Moving beyond the physical world into the spiritual world enabled me to deal with my grief.

Piet glanced at me, and I reached out to touch him. My fingers were relaxed, elegant, and fragile. He reached out to me, yet we did not physically touch. Still, I could feel the blood flow to the tips of my graceful fingers. His presence was so real, yet so ghost-like.

Feelings of numbness and depression took over my entire body. The pain of my loss was so real and complicated. I was struck with an intense state of mourning, making me realize that I had not accepted his death. I had yearned for his loving touch. I had imagined that he was alive and denied death. Tears rolled down my cheeks like a tsunami rushing to shore. My emotions were like a roller coaster ride. My world had turned upside down. Crying became exhausting. Grief had taken over my emotional and physical body. Our eyes met and I felt his comfort. He helped me through the pathway of healing through telepathy. I wanted to feel his hold and his grip. My wailing rage turned into passive resignation. His presence was monumental, and I hungered for his touch and love.

I overburdened myself with crying. My grief knew no schedule. It was uncontrollable. Yet Piet evoked a sense of joy and happiness in me. The overwhelming emotions came to a sudden halt when I heard him softly whisper, "Don't cry!"

His voice was so static., as if it came out of a radio station that was out off range.

"Someday we will be together…together *gether.*"

Time disappeared. The fog had lifted and so did my spirit. I embarked on a tour of the spiritual world. There was a crystal clear vision of Piet. He was surrounded by bright White angelic figures. They looked like a traditional church choir, all dressed in illuminated robes of white. When they sang their voices projected gloriously. I was so fascinated by their voices that I froze. They sang their original song about the end of the apartheid era.

Let's celebrate our dream,
Let's celebrate our love,
Let's celebrate our living,
Let's celebrate our dead,
Let's celebrate our freedom.
Celebrate, celebrate, celebrate!
From this heavenly kingdom
We celebrate the freedom.
Death carried us far away
On that faithful, blessed day.
From heaven we observe the change
Of a system that was so strange.
Let's celebrate our dream,
Let's celebrate our love,
Let's celebrate our living,
Let's celebrate our dead,
Let's celebrate our freedom.
Celebrate, celebrate, celebrate!
South Africa's policy a disbelief,
Created such complicated grief.
Our spirits began haunting
A government that was daunting.
We celebrate a land that's free,
A land that belongs to you and me.
Let's celebrate our dream,
Let's celebrate our love,
Let's celebrate our living,
Let's celebrate our dead,
Let's celebrate our freedom.

Celebrate, celebrate, celebrate!
Our emotions run high,
From joy we want to cry
For our rainbow nation.
From our heavenly station,
We reached out to shake your hand.
God bless our beloved land.

The gates of heaven opened in slow motion to reveal its paradise. It was almost as if it were heaven on earth. Liberated souls of eternal beauty glided towards the gate dressed in elegant white robes. A group of black church-choir singers arrived, waving the new South African flag in bright shades of green, yellow, red, blue, and deep black. On the other side, the souls of all the deceased South African rugby players, the Springboks, ascended, waving the old South African flag in the dull shades of orange, white, and blue. These white souls glared at me with fear in their eyes. Conversely, the black choir group stared with aspiration in their eyes.

It dawned on me that we were all placed in difficult circumstances. The living and the dead felt the same mixed emotions. We praised our new leader for being a peacemaker. We were elevated by his presence. Yet we were thrown into a hostile situation with intensity, believing in forty-two million South Africans. Both the living and the dead worried about revenge by those vindictive in nature.

I heard the continuous beating of Zulu drums. It sounded like the heartbeat of all South Africans. The beat of the drums echoed the mood of the South African community. The power of the drums echoed deep emotions in me. It gave me the power to touch the souls of my loved ones who had departed years ago. With each beat of the drums, I felt a sense of belonging. I felt the rhythm of life. At the same time, it connected me with the dead.

I longed to go back to sleep. I felt an ecstatic seizure as the drums continued to beat. My body articulated what it wanted to say. My head and limbs swayed to the beat. My mind, body, and soul were suddenly awakened by the sight of the most beautiful green meadows beyond the gates of heaven. It was a divine place. I traded all my fears for love and peace as I gazed beyond. The meadows were adorned with rows of marigold flowers in bright shades of yellow, orange, and red.

The flowers' scent was extremely pungent, as if to keep away any evil spirits. I could not restrict my sense of smell. Neither could I edit the beautiful scent of the marigolds. I could not resort to any mental restraints as the scent of the flowers overpowered my senses. It overwhelmed me.

Suddenly, from beyond those meadows, appeared my paternal and maternal grandparents, long deceased, followed by other family members who were long gone. They floated around chanting mantras from the Hindu scriptures. They performed a little ritual to celebrate the end of the apartheid era. They chanted in spiritual whispers, "Om shaanti, shaanti, shaanti! Lead our beloved country from darkness in light. Om peace, peace, peace." They chanted with pride. "It's all over, over, over. Your children will experience the new beginnings. A life of peace and prosperity. Let's rejoice to a future filled with peace."

A bright white orb appeared and moved stealthily around my deceased loved ones. It evoked my sense of sight. The orb changed into a figure as I watched without haste. A chubby and tall man with caramel skin appeared on horseback, like a medieval king. His black hair was brushed back, neat and tidy. His handsome smile lit up the night. Over his horse hung a blue satin sash with bold, gold letters that read THE PRIDE OF PERSIA. I perceived that it was a racehorse. I immediately recognized him, as a family member. Warmth penetrated my soul. His hand reached out to me, and I felt a bolt of lightning. It penetrated my body and dissolved in me like an asteroid sent to earth. I felt his unconditional love. He was old with wisdom and grace. The lightning bolt was a flash of luck that integrated with every muscle of my body. The horseman delivered the very essence of luck to me. His voice came out as a sweet melody: "I tried but I died!" It was a secret code that brought me a sense of love, security, and eternal fulfillment.

I felt a sudden vibration of joy and love. I reached out to touch his physical body., but he lingered far behind. I felt the nerve endings of my fingers tingle, yet I could not feel their physical touch. Tears streamed down my cheeks as a voice whispered, "Don't cry we are all fine!"

It was a vibrating whisper as Piet stepped forward. I continued to reach out, and the tips of my fingers felt more sensitive. I tricked my brain into believing that I could touch him. The black choir, the Springbok rugby team, the Zulu drummers, and my deceased family members surrounded him.

"We are here to celebrate the end of the apartheid era" came a vibration from beyond.

Piet glanced at me with tenderness and love. I felt such a, complex emotion, one I had never felt before. The feeling of strong affection together with personal attachment surrounded me. I felt the unselfish compassion of love. The intimacy of romantic love took control of me. That spiritual bond was present. The other souls looked on at our strong conviction. Piet's love was haunting and addictive, comforting and soothing.

The tune of Andy Williams's "Love Story" filled the atmosphere as Piet stretched his arm out to me. His pale white fingers pointed towards my heart. Like a laser beam, his love touched me. The black choir group began to hum the tune.

Piet's voice came out like he was singing from the heart. His voice was sweet music to my ears.

Where do I begin
To tell the story of how great love can be,

Piet's voice touched my heart, and I felt each word fill my soul with love. He withdrew his reach. He implanted the words deep down in me. A bright white light appeared in the background. The image of Piet began to fade away. I reached out to grab him. He blended with the background and was soon transparent. I raised my arm in slow motion to wave. Like an animated picture, he faded away into thick mist. Physically, Piet had departed, but spiritually he'd planted a seed in my heart. That left me content.

"Farewell, until we meet again in happier times," vibrated the whisper of the others as they bid their final farewell. "We are joyful that it's over…over…over…over…"

A bright blue light appeared, and they passed through its veil. My beloved deceased family members vanished.

I looked down and saw my horizontal body on the bed fast asleep. I felt my spirit being sucked through a silver vacuum and into my body. I woke up the next morning to find a white bird's feather on the pillow next to me. I smiled as I felt a sense of truth and wisdom.

CHAPTER 14

Peace of Mind

All things wrong turned right. Life's momentum moved me in a positive direction. I gazed up at the sky and observed a blue helium balloon float by with the words HAPPY BIRTHDAY inscribed on it. How could I miss the subtle message? That day was my birthday. It gave me some insight into the spiritual world and helped me look beyond the universe. The residue of my past suffering had subsided. The present moment became productive. I felt a radiant light and paid tribute to those boundless spirits that had brought me peace of mind.

I saw a single brown rabbit wandering around my garden. It stared at me with its beady black eyes. It approached me as a symbol of new birth, a renewal of life. Since my spiritual experience with Piet, each time a new challenge presented itself to me, a mysterious rabbit appeared, as if alerting me to face my fears. I could not paralyze my growth and movement into my future. As this rabbit locked eyes with me, I felt an instant telepathy. He conveyed the message that I am the creator of my unique thoughts and erratic emotions. I wondered if the rabbit sightings were an affirmation from the spiritual world to think positively. I felt the rabbit's vibration, and it jolted me back to reality. My fears came into focus. The rabbit inspired me to redirect my path and materialize my dreams.

I plodded in the direction of my bed, from the window. I reached out for my diary, my friend. My written words were therapeutic.

> *Dear Diary,*
> *Transported to a spiritual domain,*
> *Spirits modest and never vain,*
> *My body in a strange trance,*
> *Paranormal world where spirits advance,*
> *Spirits of the departed in plight*
> *Morphed into shape last night.*
> *Lurking in the meadows so green,*
> *Heaven a place where they are seen,*
> *Celebrating the end of the apartheid era*
> *That brought an end to such terror,*
> *A realm viewed with such disbelief,*
> *A sphere that brought me such relief,*
> *The departed souls brought me love,*
> *Placed it around my heart like a glove.*

Dear Diary, how do I visually explain
Walking down this heavenly lane?
It was not just a fabricated dream
Observing the Springbok rugby team,
Freedom songs by the black church choir.
Society would call me a pathological liar.
Orbs that projected a spiritual light
In an atmosphere that was so bright,
Spiritual mantras that were chanted.
Life on earth we take for granted,
A domain where there is no foe,
A place where eventually we will go.
Spiritual guides provide us with protection,
A place that shows absolutely no rejection.
I recall the slender spiritual staircase,
A rainbow illuminating every race.
At first I felt like a jumbo shrimp
As I progressed with a fearful limp
Smoky shadows danced around
As I levitated above the ground,
My body horizontal on my bed,
As I entered the land of the dead.
They reached out to touch my soul,
My heart is what they really stole.
Dear Diary, this is my anecdote,
Just watching all the spirits float.
The spirit of Piet visited my room,
Roaming from his spiritual tomb.
He visited me from a world beyond
With feelings so loving and fond.
I reached out to touch his hand
In this unbelievable spiritual land.

Assuring me that he is at rest
In an angelic land he knows best,
He gave me that piece of mind
And security that is hard to find.
Celebrating South African peace,
Watching all discrimination cease,
Dear Diary, his image was so vivid
As my body felt so livid.
I was given the gift of luck,
From these spirits I did not duck,
An experience that changed my life,
A story that is just so rife.
Dear Diary, I have to say thank you,
Depending on you when I feel blue.
With you I cannot feel tense,
My confessions are really so dense!

My diary proved to be a nonjudgmental confidante. It held the key to my past. It opened the door to my future. It was a powerful tool that embraced my secrets. It had a powerful impact on my frame of thought. Recording those sensational events reduced my stress levels and helped me maintain a balanced life. My diary allowed me to be analytical and rational. I knew that if I shared my experience in the paranormal world with friends, I would see eyeballs twirling like classical dancers. My spiritual enlightenment removed my entire mental blockage. The notation of seeing Piet in the spiritual world helped me release the intensity of my painful emotions. I was able to put my past dilemmas to rest. The spiritual world brought me protection and peace of mind.

When I placed my diary beside my bed, I thought I saw a shadow in the corner of my eye. I wondered if it was an optical illusion or just my fatigued state of mind. At the entrance to my room, I witnessed a full-body apparition. It was the ghostly image of a slender, petite, old Indian man. His gleaming, ghostly image caught my eye. He was a distinguished old man, clad in a white loincloth. He was brown and wore round, gold-rimmed eyeglasses. He was bald and frail. I knew it was no hoax. I heard his disembodied voice say, "Thank you! God bless South Africa!"

He placed his palms together, as if praying. I understood that this was his sense of respect. He was my solid, irrefutable knowledge of paranormal activity beyond. I felt an adrenaline rush as the apparition of this great Indian leader faded away. The visits of the spirits from beyond enabled me to attain closure.

Biography

Born in Durban, South Africa, **Kass Ghayouri** immigrated to Canada in 1989. Her vow of selfless service has led her to teach at schools in South Africa and various secondary schools in Toronto, Canada. With conventional wisdom and studious work habits, she is able to juggle two jobs as a twelfth grade English teacher and coowner of a tutorial school, **Governess Academy** in Markham, Ontario, with her husband. She graduated with bachelor of arts degrees in English and psychology. She attained postgraduate degrees in English and school guidance and counseling. Her professional career outside of academia includes writing poetry and novels and illustrating. She tutors university students, helping them review complex course materials. She helps them convey ideas succinctly by editing their dissertations, master's theses, term papers, and admission essays for accuracy and clarity. As a fourth-generation Indian South African, she endured and lived through one of the most brutal legacies of the apartheid era. The remnants of colonialism impacted her culture, tradition, heritage, and lifestyle.

An Era of Error is her second novel and unique footprint on this planet. **An Era of Error** falls into the genre of historic fiction and is based on the apartheid era in South Africa. It explores profound issues, which the reader is engaged to analyze. Its chronological scope is evident in its context, which is focused yet flexible. The plot transports the reader through a window of deeper insight into the life of an Indian female growing up during the apartheid regime in South Africa. Kass Ghayouri provides the reader the opportunity to witness the huge obstacles her characters face living in South Africa during the apartheid era. Each reader has the majestic power to delve into that moment and experience the brutal force of the book's thrilling plot. Her first novel is **The Fugitive's Baby.**

20099569R00113

Made in the USA
Charleston, SC
27 June 2013